M000234064

The Enchanted Lands of

Norway

A Zaria Fierce Novel

Aleks Mickelsen and the Twice-Lost Fairy Well

By Keira Gillett

Dear Kaitlin,

Welcome to the fierce team! Your map is stunning. Thank you for bringing your art and talents to my world.

♡ Keira Gillett

Reading Order:

Praise for Zaria Fierce and the Secret of Gloomwood Forest

"Are you in the mood for an old-fashioned magical jaunt? Zaria Fierce and the Secret of Gloomwood Forest by Keira Gillett is a classic "perilous adventure" book for middle grade readers." *Jennifer Bardsley, The YA Gal*

"A captivating blending of fantasy storytelling with today's technology. At the base of this tale is deep, abiding friendship that stands the tests of time, adventure and even danger." *Kathy Haw, Goodreads Review*

"If you're looking for an action-packed adventure dipped in fantasy, look no further. This book kept me on my toes with its many cliffhangers and plot twists; it was quite hard to put down at times." *Meredith, All 'Bout Them Books and Stuff*

"This was a really good book with a great setting and cool plot line. I really liked how it didn't hide that Zaria was adopted and she knew it. I also liked how her adoptive parents were nice. You don't see that often in books (as an adopted kid, I like it when adoption is portrayed well)." *Erik, This Kid Reviews Books*

"A great book with vivid descriptions and relatable characters. The main character becomes a strong female lead, and the writing and illustrations make this fantasy world even more real and interesting." *Analee, Book Snacks*

Praise for Zaria Fierce and the Enchanted Drakeland Sword

"The Zaria Fierce series just keeps getting better with this sequel! This is an awesome fantasy filled with suspense, from the first page to the last! The vivid descriptions, combined with the beautiful illustrations, make the setting come to life." *Brandi Nyborg, Goodreads Review*

"This is one of the most amazing second books in a trilogy that I've read. I like how empowering the book is, especially on facing your own demons. Just like Zaria." *Danissa, The Booklandia*

"I like how the action begins quickly and Gillett brings the reader up to speed on the plot, no time is wasted in getting these friends off on another adventure through the Norwegian countryside. Oh, and that setting, it's one of the most enjoyable things in reading Gillett's stories. All the lovely, rich, details of each of the magical kingdoms, each place is unique and highlights the depth of her imagination." *Brenda, Log Cabin Library*

"Zaria is both vulnerable and strong, and very much a role model for my own daughters." *APinFL, Audible Review*

Praise for Zaria Fierce and the Dragon Keeper's Golden Shoes

"That's the great thing about the Zaria Fierce trilogy: adventure is fast, furious, and loaded with Norse mythology, but the friendship between Zaria and her group of friends is the heart that drives this story." *Rosemary, Mom Read It*

"*Zaria Fierce and the Dragon Keeper's Golden Shoes* was the magical conclusion this trilogy asked for. Filled with action and adventure, Zaria and her friends showed us the importance of teamwork, friendship, and having courage in ourselves. The perfect ending to a fun series, I recommend this to all fantasy lovers, middle school and beyond!" *Emily, Midwestern Book Nerd*

"*Zaria Fierce and the Dragon Keeper's Golden Shoes* was a spectacular conclusion to a great trilogy (though the ending left the door open for more adventures). Filled with magic, a great story line, amazing and real characters, wonderful settings and beautifully explored themes, Keira Gillett created a trilogy that I will always cherish and will visit anytime. If you like The Chronicles of Narnia, The Hobbit, The Spiderwick Chronicles or simply love a book filled with Norwegian folklore and fantasy, then this is the ultimate series for you to read, devour and lose yourselves in." *Ner, A Cup of Coffee and a Book*

Dedication:

I dedicate this sequel to Zaria Fierce to my dad. He is the sweetest, most supportive father. Thank you for encouraging me to pursue my dreams.

Acknowledgements:

This book could not have been put together without the incredible generosity and support of these amazing people. Your enthusiasm and kindness are invaluable and very dear to me. Thank you for everything. May all your adventures be fierce!

Karin Gillett, Sara Jennings, Sharon Fletcher, Shawn Meyer, Karen Oates, Kevin Gillett, Megan Donahue Hahn, Shawn Alexander, and Alisha Jefferson

To Readers:

Whether, you are new to the world of Zaria Fierce, or a longtime fan of the trilogy, thank you for picking up this book. It's readers like you who make a fandom great. I hope you enjoy this continuance of the story. We'll be following a certain changeling as he navigates his way through what lies ahead. Watch out for the dragons. They bite. Wishing you safe journeys and much adventure!

Table of Contents

Prologue: The Changeling

Aleks Mickelsen preferred being a normal teenage boy. He didn't like to stick out, which unfortunately for him, he did. A lot. It's bound to happen when one has bright red-orange hair, a mass of freckles, and slightly pointy ears. The ears, he thought with a grimace, were a holdover from his fey heritage. Something he tried to ignore most days. He didn't like either of them – his ears or the fey.

The whole fairy kingdom with its four courts, from his older siblings, to his ruling father, to the species in general, made him sick. He was glad he was a changeling and that they had gotten rid of him. The longer he stayed with his human family, the more human he became, which was something he desperately wanted. Soon, he would become fully human. The day couldn't come fast enough.

According to his grams he would become human if he stayed with his human family to his majority. For fairies this was at the age of sixteen. How did his grams know this? Coincidentally, Ava Mickelsen, too, was a changeling. Or, perhaps, not so coincidentally.

Amongst the fey, Ava was Grimkell's aunt. Because Grimkell was his birth father, this made her Aleks' great-aunt. On his human side, she was his paternal grandmother. His father, Samuel Mickelsen, and his mother, Naia, weren't his actual parents, although they didn't know that. To them, he was their natural-born child. Such is the life of a changeling.

Most days Aleks chose to ignore the complications – not to mention the confusion – of his origin and family. He didn't care about his fairy heritage. Only his human.

It is most unusual for the fey to place two changelings into the same human family, let alone two changelings from the same fairy family into the same human family. Aleks never questioned why he had been inserted into the Mickelsen's; he was simply grateful for it.

Over the last year, Grams had tried to talk him out of his plans for his majority, because unlike what Aleks planned to do, Ava had chosen to keep some of her fairy magic. She had left her human home one week before her majority on a school trip, which allowed her to keep a little of her fairy magic.

It wasn't much, but she used her magic to grow splendid, fairy-like gardens around her home. The gardens always burst with color, being loaded with blossoms right up to the first wintery day with snow on the ground. They were also the first to bloom after the snow melted in the spring.

Aleks' innate magical ability was his sense of direction. He never got lost. He always knew which way to go in any situation. It had been very useful two years ago when fighting against a shapeshifting dragon named Koll. In the years since, not so much.

His friend, Zaria Fierce, was a sorceress of enormous power, which surprised everyone who took her at face value. On the outside she was the shy, bookworm type. By the end of that adventure, however, she had grown more confident and bold, even slaying a dragon. He could only imagine what Zaria felt when facing down the oldest of the dragon brothers. He still shuddered at the memories of his encounter with Koll's younger brother, Egil.

The younger dragon had a voice like a wildcat's growl. Its eerie quality had raised the hairs on his skin, causing him to tremble in fear. The voice had been so at odds with the pleasant looking man who'd appeared out of the shadows. When he'd shifted to his dragon form, Egil had a forked tongue and scales so fine, they moved like fur on a wolf.

Pushing away the memory, Aleks got out of bed, grateful they had recaptured Koll's brother. He wouldn't want Queen Helena's job guarding the dragons. She was Zaria's birth mother and ruled the Under Realm, a prison designed by the different magical species using what talents they had to contribute to its effectiveness.

Looking out his bedroom window, he absently touched his ears, feeling the pointy juncture on the top. When he was younger, his ears stuck out like sore thumbs. Kids had teased him, until one day, a short, skinny boy, dressed like he was going to church instead of school, stepped in and pushed one of the kids down into the dirt, scattering the rest of them.

After that, the boy, Geirr Engelstad, and Aleks became fast friends, and over time, to his vast relief, his ears rounded out, becoming less and less noticeable. He still wore his hair a little long, though, to cover them. No sense calling unwanted attention to their shape. If he'd heard one Spock joke, he'd heard them all.

In one short month, he'd be sixteen, and if he was smart, fully human. He'd met Grimkell, his fairy siblings, Nori and Lukas, and his cousin Isak during the adventures to fight Koll. Having met his fey family, Aleks wanted nothing to do with them and their backbiting ways.

He'd been lucky to escape with his life. Changelings were usually killed on the spot if found back inside the Niffleheim, a void which housed the four fairy courts. Luckily for him, Zaria had tricked Grimkell into a favor to ensure the safety of all her friends and passage out of Niffleheim to Jerndor, home of the dwarves. She and her champions were able to win three matches of intelligence, endurance, and strength by the skin of their teeth, – and a little non-personal magic – and he'd been safe.

The time was coming when he could – and would – leave it all behind. His ears would be as round as anyone else's and his ability, which he would miss just a little if he was honest with himself, would be lost. A small price to pay for something he'd wished for as long as he could remember.

And really, he wouldn't be needed again to fight dragons. Zaria had slain Koll, and his only compatriot and brother had been recaptured. Egil wasn't a threat. His time traipsing peripatetically around Norway was over. His days now were normal, slow, and boring. That's the way he liked it. Truly. All he wanted was a nice, ordinary, human life. There wouldn't be any more adventures for him, or for his friends.

Or so he thought.

Chapter One: Things Fall Apart

At first, Aleks didn't notice anything out of the ordinary about his day as he walked to school. In hindsight, he really should have noticed the signs that today was going to be a strange day. To be fair though, it had started innocently enough.

In the morning, his mom hadn't been able to find her keys. Aleks found them in the fridge of all places. He was grateful for his innate navigational ability in times like this, because who knew how long they would have had to search to find them otherwise. Naia Mickelsen wasn't normally a forgetful person, so

Aleks chalked it up to a stressful week, and the presentation she was hurrying to finish for work.

Then, as he caught up with Geirr and Filip for school, the tranquil morning was broken by screeching tires and spastic honking as two cars nearly collided with each other. He and his friends talked about that for a moment, remarking on the skid marks on the road, before returning their conversation to their math homework.

Aleks hated homework. He thought it was a waste of time, but luckily for him he had the stargazer, a device shaped like an egg and covered in star cutouts. When he felt pushed for time he could activate the device and instantly get some of it back. It also had another function: if he pressed a different button, it would act as a flashlight in the dark.

Grams was the one who gave him the handy little device. Over the course of their adventures it had proven to be a particularly powerful stargazer. He and his friends had discovered that it could freeze time, not just in the small space of someone's home, but also across an entire city. That had been something to see! It also allowed them all to sneak off without their parents being the wiser.

The magic and mechanics behind the stargazer were a little fuzzy and Aleks was glad he'd never have to build one. It was enough to know that when activated, time froze for humans and non-magical creatures who were not touching the device, or who were not touching somebody touching the device. To keep everyone alert and unfrozen, Aleks and his friends had made many a human chain.

Magical beings weren't frozen. Aleks assumed this was because their innate magic resisted the device's magic. Zaria, as a sorceress, couldn't be frozen. Aleks, as a changeling, and soon to be human, could be frozen. Technically, he still had magic, and a part of him thought he, like Zaria, shouldn't be affected. And yet, because the stargazer could work on him, it meant he was nearing his ultimate goal.

If one was frozen, time would seem to pass somewhat normally; but when the device was deactivated, that same person would feel as if time had flown by. This played tricks on people's memories, but was very handy when one wanted to get chores done in one's own sweet time. Not that Aleks would ever use the device for such a purpose.

He felt a little guilty looking at Geirr as his friend scrambled to get four math problems completed before the morning bell. He'd used the stargazer last night to get in some extra video game time before bed, which would have robbed Geirr of valuable time to do homework. This morning, his friend was a complete mess.

Geirr's normally smart appearance looked haphazard. His collar and cuffs were unbuttoned, and half of his shirt dangled untucked from his pants. Aleks wondered if his selfish use of the stargazer was the reason he wasn't finished. Then he remembered Geirr hated math with a passion and would probably look like this anyway, after spending a rough night trying to get it completed.

When the pencil tip broke, Geirr cursed and threw it aside. He stuffed his homework into the book and shoved it into his backpack. "I freaking hate algebra."

"It's not so bad," Zaria said, appearing on their left. Their mutual friend, Christoffer was with her. "What are you missing? Maybe I can help."

Geirr shook his head. "I don't care anymore. I've got bigger things to worry about."

"Like what?" Christoffer asked.

"Where were you this morning? You were supposed to come by my place to complete our report for Mr. Larsen's class," Aleks said.

Christoffer shrugged his backpack higher. "It's the strangest thing. I didn't quite know how to get there. One minute I knew where I was, and the next everything looked different. Then I ran into Zaria and forgot all about it."

"That's odd," Aleks managed before Geirr cut in.

"I've got my first flight this afternoon using my private pilot's license," he said excitedly. "I'm so happy I passed and got it last week. You don't know how long it took to persuade my mom to let me do it. If she hadn't agreed, I'd still be waiting to get it."

"Hi, Zar-Zar," Filip said, unconsciously giving her cow eyes. "How are you?"

She flashed him a warm smile. "I'm great. I just started this new book –"

Aleks watched them as they walked across the school campus. He knew his friend had a massive crush on the sorceress. Objectively, he could see why. Zaria was smart, compassionate, and capable of producing a mean apple cake just by thinking about it. That last bit wasn't even hyperbolic. She really could conjure up a mean apple cake just by thinking about it.

She was also kind of pretty, with big, purple eyes, soft, creamy bronze skin, and long, dark hair. She used to wear it in twin braids, and while she still wore braids, she usually did a girly updo with it, like today, where it wrapped around her head like a crown or a wreath and exposed her long neck.

Filip, on the other hand, was more awkward than anything else, especially around her. He'd grown a foot taller and still didn't know quite what to do with his hands and feet. He was prone to tripping over thresholds and knocking over cups, which meant his friends gave him a wide berth at the lunch table. It frustrated Filip beyond anything, because he prided himself on being a good athlete.

He had an edgy, blond haircut that dipped into his green eyes, which Geirr's slightly older sister, Kajsa, had once called dreamy. Aleks wondered what Zaria thought of Filip when she looked at him. Did she think his eyes were dreamy too? Would this semester be the one when Filip finally got up the nerve to ask her out? He'd have to wait and see.

A new voice greeted them as they entered the school. "Good morning, everyone. May I take your bag, Princess?"

Aleks looked up and spied Henrik, the newest member of their friend group. Henrik, previously known to them as Hart (or the spare), was now the Stag Lord of the ellefolken, which made him a prince and heir-apparent. He was Filip's biggest competition for Zaria's attentions, or at least that's how Filip felt. Aleks wasn't so sure. It was sometimes hard to read their enigmatic friend.

Henrik was a little shorter than Filip, with pale brown hair and shockingly blue eyes, almost like Geirr's. Kajsa called them cobalt, when she'd met him the first time. The teen's hairstyle matched Filip's, or perhaps, more accurately, Filip's hairstyle matched Henrik's, whose locks slashed across his forehead and made girls swoon as they passed.

"You shouldn't call her that at school," Christoffer said, elbowing him. "You're going to draw unwanted attention. Plus, all the girls will think you're dating her and then how will you be my wingman?"

Christoffer was the heart of the group. He was the funny one, outgoing, and bright-eyed. He'd loved exploring magical Norway and couldn't understand Aleks' reticence toward it. As the son of Chinese immigrants, he was good at fitting in wherever he was, and his laid-back happy attitude won him many friends and kept them, too.

His mother taught history at the lower secondary level, and his father was a doctor. He had two younger sisters, twins, who were holy terrors. Aleks knew this from helping Christoffer babysit them on occasion. For a time, that was the only way Christoffer had been allowed to hang out with his friends, until his parents realized that his disappearance nearly three years ago wasn't going to be repeated. After all, how often does one get kidnapped by a troll?

Aleks winced, recalling more than one tea party with the twins. He'd never drunk so much *tea* in his life. The indignity of having to do so while wearing a pink feather boa, blue eye shadow, and tons of costume jewelry just rubbed more salt into the wound. Christoffer loved them, which is why Aleks put up with it, but he swore never to use the stargazer with the girls. No sense in prolonging the torture.

The bell rang, and the group splintered off, going in multiple directions: Aleks and Filip to language studies, Zaria and Henrik to chemistry for lab work, Geirr to algebra, and Christoffer to world history. They promised to meet up at lunch and talk about plans for after school. The weekend was upon them, and they had decisions to make.

"He's always by her side," Filip said glumly, looking over his shoulder as Zaria and Henrik disappeared around the corner.

"Why don't you just ask her out?" Aleks countered, dodging a group of girls coming at them in the hall. They always seemed to travel in packs, congesting traffic wherever they went.

"Didn't you listen? He's always by her side. I can't get her away from him. He just tags along."

"That's because Zaria convinced her parents to host a foreign exchange student. She got them to sign the paperwork. He lives with her."

"I know. And I've hated it ever since she brought him home after Koll was defeated," Filip said, rolling his eyes. "I still can't believe her parents bought that he was from Denmark."

Aleks shrugged. "They're American. They don't know better, and anyway, she was the only one who could get him into the school, passing him off as an army brat to the administration."

Filip sighed. "I know, I know. It just sucks. He's always around, calling her princess, making her laugh. I don't know what to do."

Aleks clapped him on the shoulder and steered him into the classroom just as the second bell rang. "He's a prince who can have only one heir and mates for life with the girl who gives him said offspring. That's not really a recipe for romance. You'll be fine."

Filip gave him a wry look. "You'd be surprised, mate, just what – or who – girls like."

"Gentlemen, please take your seats," said Mrs. Berg, their teacher, as the door shut behind them.

Aleks sat down and pulled out his textbook and notebook, placing them on the table he shared with Filip. Clicking his pen, he settled into the lecture on sentence construction, copying the phrases on the board, with Filip dutifully doing the same beside him.

The hour passed quickly. This was unusual for school, where the hours seemed to drag. When it seemed like a day would never end, Aleks wondered if the teachers had their own stargazers. They would be diabolical enough to use them, too, if they did.

It helped that Mrs. Berg was a very dynamic teacher who got her students involved. Her classes never failed to entertain. Absorbed as he was in the lecture, Aleks at first didn't notice anything. Then something acrid hit his nose, jolting him from his note taking.

"FIRE," cried a girl by the windows. "Look, over there!"

His gaze followed where she pointed. While other students crowded around her, blocking his view, Aleks stood up on his chair. Looking through the window, he watched black smoke billow out of two windows on the other side of campus.

"That's the chemistry lab," Filip said, shoving back his chair.

Mrs. Berg cut in front of Filip, blocking his exit. Clapping her hands together, she drew all the kids away from the windows and formed them into a line.

"Students, stick together," Mrs. Berg admonished as the fire alarm started blaring. "Hurry now. Stay orderly. No shoving."

She led them from the classroom, merging them into the stream of students pouring out into the halls.

Many students hadn't yet realized it wasn't a fire drill, as they were gossiping and checking their smart phones. When they reached the double exit doors, propped open, the gossiping turned into excited shouts, as everyone began to realize there was an actual fire on campus.

"We have to get over there," Filip called back, shoving his way through the crowd. "Zaria and Henrik could be in trouble."

"Filip, stop. No, Filip. Stop!" shouted Aleks, pushing through bodies to catch up. "You can't go toward the fire."

Sirens blared in the distance. For a second, Aleks watched as fire engines made their way across the river. He glanced back to find Filip and saw that he was gone. Swearing, Aleks pushed harder and forced his way through the throng. He slipped between bodies and stumbled out into an opening, gasping and choking on the smoke that suddenly blew toward him, stinging his eyes.

In the distance, Filip raced across the green toward the other crowd of students.

"Come on, man," Aleks grumbled, and took off after him, ignoring the shouts of teachers telling him to turn around.

He sprinted, putting on speed and leaping over a ditch to follow Filip. As he approached, he searched for the others, using his innate navigational sense to locate them in the crowd of dirty students. He spied Henrik first, standing a foot taller than the girls that clustered near him. On his left stood Zaria, clutching a book. Some things never changed.

"Filip," he called, pointing at them. "Over there!"

"Zaria!" shouted Filip, skidding to a halt in front of her. He grabbed her shoulders and gave her a small shake. "Are you okay? Are you hurt anywhere?"

She shook her head, clutching her book tighter. "I'm fine. Henrik got me out."

Filip's mouth tightened slightly, but he nodded to the Stag Lord. "It's good then that you were there. Are you okay, mate?"

"I'm fine," Henrik said. "There was a lot of smoke –"

"Still is," Aleks said, indicating the black clouds spilling out of the lower floor of the building.

Just then, the fire engines pulled up and a team of firefighters took over the scene. Men were deployed to walk the building's perimeter, hand lines were advanced and unkinked, apparatuses and tools were set up, and water was connected. Like clockwork, the team took up their positions and aimed. Nozzles opened, and the fire was attacked at its source, cutting off its extension.

"What happened?" asked Filip, as they watched the firefighters operate the hoses.

"A Bunsen burner exploded in the chemistry lab across the hall," said Zaria. "Or at least that's what the others are saying."

"Seriously? What were they working with?" asked Aleks. "Dragon fire?"

School administrators with tablets cut through the masses assembled and started roll calling. Kids shouted "Here!" as they heard their names, and they were checked off the roster. Aleks and Filip stayed and did the same, as their names were called.

Working swiftly and methodically, the firefighters brought order to the chaos. The fire was quickly extinguished, and the students were dismissed for the rest of the day. The unexpected early release was greeted with cheers from all around. Aleks and the others gravitated toward the front of campus, looking for Geirr and Christoffer. When they met up, Geirr's eyes were alight with excitement.

"This is great, guys," he said, slinging his backpack up and over his arm. "I can go do my flight early. Does anybody want to come along? I can take two, maybe three with me. It's not like flying on the back of a winter-wyvern, but it's still pretty cool. I can show you the sights."

"I'll go," said Aleks. "I liked it the last time I was up. I'm not doing anything and my folks will be at work."

"We're supposed to help Mrs. Fierce with household work today," said Henrik, his voice wistful.

Zaria nodded, looking disappointed. "I'd love to go, but we've got chores and dinner preparations to do. An early start means we'll be able to hang out later."

"My parents don't want me doing anything dangerous," said Christoffer, somewhere between rueful and apologetic. "They'd say going up with you is like going out in a car with a first-time driver. Besides, I have to go find mum soon and let her know I'm okay. This sort of thing worries her."

"I can go," said Filip. "It's Friday after all, so why not? I have the whole weekend to do my science homework. It'll be fun."

Little did they know what would happen next.

Chapter Two: An Unexpected Visitor

The mid-morning flight was exhilarating. To Aleks it felt like freedom, and he could see why Geirr loved it so much. The aerial views were breathtaking. In fact, it had been such a pleasant experience, Aleks wished it didn't have to end. He was already wondering when he could press Geirr to take him up again.

He sat behind the copilot seat of a Cessna 182, enjoying the view. Filip sat beside him, nose pressed to the window. Svein, a fellow pilot who had some free time and came along for the ride, sat in the copilot seat. He and Geirr had been excellent tour guides, telling them where to look and what they were looking at. It had been a beautiful clear afternoon.

Now they were approaching the airport, preparing to land and grab a late lunch. Aleks was proud of his friend's accomplishment. Geirr had wanted this for years, and now he was licensed and could go up more often. He was saving for his own aircraft, thinking he might want to start a business air taxiing people around Norway.

The ground rose up, coming close. Aleks could see the crisscrossing runways get bigger and bigger. A button lit up on the control panel.

"What does DH mean?" asked Filip, pointing to it.

"Decision height," said Svein, looking back. "Geirr must decide whether he can make the landing or must execute a go-around to try his approach again."

Geirr checked his instruments and distance to the runway. He nodded. "This will be a piece of cake," he said. "Just like practice."

The plane lowered steadily. Aleks and Filip watched the ground. Geirr sat in the pilot seat, relaxed and carefree, talking to them about what he was doing.

In an instant, the smooth landing soured. Out of nowhere, a strong gust of wind blew sideways at them, botching the approach. It was too late to shift course. Geirr called out to Svein, who grabbed at the controls. Aleks shouted in alarm, bracing himself against the seat ahead, instinctively knowing what was about to happen.

Split-seconds later the plane crashed heavily into the grass adjacent to the runway. The right side bore the brunt of the landing, causing the landing gear to snap, tipping the plane sideways. Aleks grabbed at the seat in front of him, as the propeller hit against the ground.

They skidded through the dirt, the aluminum steel fuselage groaning horribly as it absorbed the impact. Air trapped in Aleks' lungs, as he waited with bated breath to see if the aircraft would flip over. A loud groan shivered through the aircraft, and the plane thumped down.

As the shuddering and groaning came to a halt, Aleks let out the breath he'd been holding with a whoosh. Svein clicked off his restraint and shoved at the door.

"Door's stuck," he said. "How's everybody doing? Anyone hurt?"

"I'm fine," Aleks said.

"Me too," said Filip. "Geirr?"

They looked at him, but Geirr didn't move. Filip tried to rouse him. He was knocked out. Svein cursed and grabbed for the old-fashioned window opener, which looked like it belonged in an eighties' car, not on an aircraft. He cracked open the window a few inches, but then it stuck.

"It won't budge," he growled, leaning his weight into the crank, trying to fully extend the window. "We need to get out of here."

"What are we going to do?" asked Aleks.

"I have to get to that little arm and break it," said Svein, pointing to the corner of the window. "If the window had opened all the way I could have kicked the arm to break it."

"Try kicking the window," suggested Filip.

Svein nodded and turned sideways in his seat. Leaning back, he lifted his legs and kicked. His feet landed with a dull *thunk*. The window was a hard plastic material, not glass, for safety. It took several blows to get it to budge. Svein then kicked at the arm, snapping it. He caught the window as it fell down.

The sound of sirens, faint in the distance, signaled the approach of emergency vehicles. With a grunt, Svein pushed himself out of the plane. He landed with a thump on the ground. The crenellated wing above his head was a daunting reminder of how close they had come to tipping over.

"Everyone out. Now!" he shouted, indicating for Filip to climb through.

"I can't. Not without Geirr," said Filip.

"Help me move him," Aleks ordered. "You take his arms."

They labored under their friend's weight, struggling to shift him enough in the tight space to get a good grip on him. It was a tough squeeze in the cockpit. Filip backed up toward the window and angled Geirr through the opening. Svein guided his head through and then pulled him out by his shoulders. As Geirr plopped to the ground, the engine started smoking.

"That's not good guys. You better hurry," Svein said, holding the window until Filip caught it.

Svein hauled Geirr away from the aircraft as Filip scrambled through the window. Aleks shoved his friend's legs out, which toppled Filip over. He landed in a disgruntled heap. The window banged shut. Filip popped up and lifted the window with one hand, using the other to reach in for Aleks. He gripped Filip's arms, kicking off the seat as Filip tugged hard. They just managed to keep their footing.

"Get away from the plane," shouted Svein, who was carrying Geirr in a fireman's hold. "We need to get to a safe distance."

Aleks nodded and ducked under the wing as emergency vehicles arrived at the scene. Filip quickly followed, and they raced across the grass to the opposite runway, where the vehicles were gathered. Another team of firefighters connected their hoses and stretched the lines out to the aircraft to douse the smoking engine.

Someone asked them what happened. Aleks stared blankly at Geirr's unconscious form, as Svein parsed out what had transpired. It wasn't enough. They were asked repeatedly and in different fashions what went wrong. Svein explained that he didn't know, saying that the whole event was quite unusual because Geirr was such a good pilot. He even commended Geirr for keeping a cool head when the landing went askew.

With the pilot's words in his ears, Aleks' mind whirled with the possibilities. What had gone wrong? It was true that it was unlike Geirr to miss a landing. Everything had started out smoothly enough. The plane had been lined up perfectly to the runway.

It was only when the wind burst had hit them that things went sideways. He glanced at the nearby trees; not a single leaf stirred. He frowned, feeling sweat trickle down his neck. Something wasn't right. His thoughts arrested as his friend's eyelids started fluttering.

Geirr groaned and sat up as paramedical personnel attended to him. "Is everyone all right?" he asked, holding his head.

"You're the one hit on the head, mate, not us," Filip said, smiling in relief. "Glad you're awake."

"I'm so sorry, guys," he said. "That's the first time something like this has ever happened to me."

"We're all safe," Aleks said reassuringly. "Don't stress. How's the head?"

"You did really well, kid," Svein said, coming over. "The plane didn't flip, and we're all out safe. It wasn't your fault. I've seen you land a plane hundreds of times. Don't let this get you down."

"How did you get me out?" Geirr asked, rubbing his eyes.

"The door wouldn't open," said Filip.

Aleks nodded, adding, "We went out the window. Svein, here, had to kick it and the little arm thingy, allowing it to swing open enough to let us out."

"Sometimes the doors stick on a Cessna," Geirr said. "I hope it stuck naturally and wasn't warped because of the crash."

"I couldn't tell looking at it from the outside," Svein replied. "That'll be revealed in the inspection."

"Oh no," Geirr groaned, closing his eyes. "I didn't even think of that. This sucks."

"I've got a few more questions to answer," Svein said, indicating some official looking people near the plane. "They'll come talk to you later."

"My mother will never let me fly again," Geirr moaned, as Svein walked away. "They're not going to be happy with the bill for the damages. There go all my savings. I'm going to be grounded for life."

A bark of laughter escaped Aleks. "You and Christoffer can be a matched pair."

"His mum would have killed me," Geirr said, laughing weakly. "I'm glad he wasn't in the plane."

Aleks looked back at the torn-up aircraft. "I should have had the stargazer on me. I could have stopped the crash."

"How would we have explained being outside the plane without a scratch?" Geirr asked.

Aleks shrugged. "We would have figured it out."

"There wasn't time to activate it," countered Filip. He raked a hand through his hair. "And let's say you did.

How could you have made contact with Geirr and me to keep us unfrozen? It just wasn't possible."

"And Svein," Geirr said. "How would you have explained it to him?"

"I'll keep the stargazer on me anyway from now on," said Aleks staunchly. "Just in case. I don't want to be caught unprepared again."

He looked up at the trees and sky as a wispy cool breeze blew across the back of his neck. Clouds swirled ominously, hovering as if watching the scene unfurl below. Aleks couldn't remember a single dark cloud when they were in the air. Or even a few minutes ago. Now suddenly there was a whole group of them? He didn't like it.

"Trouble is brewing," Geirr said. "First, there was the fire at school and now this."

"No," Filip said, shaking his head. "First, there were those two cars that almost collided."

"Wait, didn't Christoffer get lost on his way to Aleks'? That was first," said Geirr.

"No. First, my mom misplaced her keys in the fridge," said Aleks, thinking back to how his day started.

"Seriously? In the fridge?" Geirr asked, chuckling.

He doubled up with laughter, practically crying, like it was the funniest thing he'd ever heard. Filip gave Aleks a worried look.

"It's not that funny," he said, dubiously.

It wasn't, but it was cathartic and what Geirr needed to get him through the ordeal. Aleks understood that, so he let his friend laugh it out. Eventually, Geirr stopped. He looked miserable, as a police officer offered to escort them home.

He was dropped off first; rushed into the house by a visibly upset Mrs. Engelstad. Then Aleks was returned home. He was reluctant to get out of the vehicle and go inside. He looked at Filip, sitting with him in the back seat, then back at the officer holding the door open.

"We should tell Zaria about this, don't you think?" Filip asked.

Aleks nodded and slid out. "I'll call Christoffer and let him know. You call Zaria and Henrik."

The officer came to the door with him, to tell his parents what had happened. His dad answered. Aleks told him he was fine and slipped inside as the officer began to talk. He went straight to his bedroom and pulled out the stargazer from under his pillow and stuffed it into his pocket.

He wasn't going to take any more chances. Today was turning out to be a crazy day. What if tomorrow was worse? He sat on the bed, holding his head in his hands. He could tell he was still out of it. Nothing processed quite right.

A few moments later his father, Samuel, came in and sat down next to him, pulling him into a hug. "I'm glad you're all right. I couldn't imagine something happening to you. I called your mom. She's leaving work now and coming home."

"What about her presentation?" Aleks asked, his voice slightly muffled by his dad's shoulder. He pulled back. "I'm fine. Really."

"Still, we'll take it easy this weekend. Maybe not go camping and boating like we had planned."

Aleks sighed, feeling depressed. "I was looking forward to fishing with you and Grandpa."

"Remigus will understand," his father assured him. He grinned a little and added, "Who knows, maybe your mother will let you out of her sight, and we can still go. We'll wait and see what she says."

Aleks made a face. "That's not going to happen."

Samuel's grin widened. "Oh, I don't know. Perhaps we can convince her it'll keep you out of trouble. You seem to have a knack for getting in the middle of it today between the school and this." He ruffled Aleks' hair. "Seriously, kid. Try not to worry us again for a few weeks. We want you to make it to your sixteenth birthday."

"I want to, too," Aleks said, swatting his dad's hand away. He combed his hair down.

"I'm going to start making dinner. Take a shower and put on some clean clothes. It'll reassure your mother that you're all right."

Aleks nodded and his dad left. He plugged in his phone to charge and turned on some music. He let it pound in his ears, sinking into the depths of it, until he felt a little more human and a little less like the walking dead. His mind cleared, and he started to undress, when a sharp knock pounded on his window.

The face staring back at him was not one he expected. Usually Christoffer poked his head in at least once every other week, when he skipped out on his parents' restrictive rules. They were getting more lenient, but for Christoffer half the fun was bailing without permission.

The visitor at his window, though, wasn't Christoffer. Aleks scowled at her. She shouldn't be here. She had no reason to be here. Looking at her, Aleks wished his fey power was the ability to pulverize someone.

He threw open the window. "What are you doing here?" he demanded. "How did you get out of Niffleheim?"

Nori sniffed and tossed her long curly hair, the same orange-red as his, to the side. "The same way you and your little friends did. How else? Now, are you going to move aside and let me in, or stand there like a lump? Put your shirt back on, too. Gross. No sister wants to see that."

Aleks' nostrils flared. "You are not my sister."

She flicked one long-fingered hand at him, pushing him aside. She climbed into his room and stood up. They were nearly eye-level. The last time he had seen her, she'd stared down her pointy nose at him. She couldn't do that anymore, which made him smirk.

She sniffed at him, raising an eyebrow. She looked in distaste around his room. "Your God-awful music is enough to give anyone a headache. Turn it off, or at the very least, down."

"What do you know about human technology?" Aleks asked.

"More than I care to. Luckily they've generally found metals other than iron to use these days for their gadgets. Small favor, that."

Aleks pulled on his shirt and crossed his arms. "Why are you here?"

"Because it's time for you to come home," Nori said without a trace of malice. "You're needed, little brother."

He laughed. "Good one. No, really. Why are you here?"

Nori stared him down like a bug on her shoe. "Father's lost power. Uncle Ytorm and Aunt Cornelia have taken the throne. I always knew they couldn't be trusted. The court is in ruins. War is coming. And it's all your fault."

"My fault?" Aleks asked, his eyebrows rising nearly to his hairline. "My fault? How is it my fault?"

"Because mother let you live, and then you returned," she hissed. "Now you have to fix it, or else this war will tear Niffleheim apart."

"Good!" shouted Aleks. "Let it. Why should I care?"

Nori shook her head and sat herself gingerly on the edge of his bed. She pressed a hand to the bridge of her nose and sighed. "Of all the gifts I could have, why is it the ability to sort out the truth?"

"Truth?" Aleks asked. "Your best fairy gift is truth?"

Nori looked put out. "I know it's a horrible gift. I wish I had Lukas' gift, because I would never have let Ytorm and Cornelia win."

"What is Lukas' gift?"

"Fighting, but they drugged him with a sleeping draught and placed him in chains."

"Well, he wasn't very smart now, was he?"

She sighed in disgust. "Never. He's as dumb as rocks, which is why it goaded me so much to have to compete against him for favor with father."

"Should have kept me around instead," Aleks said dryly.

"We couldn't," Nori said. "No family is allowed to keep three kits. It's illegal. You were the youngest. I saw, with my gift, how you would be king one day, and knowing this, mother wanted you to live. I took you from her arms and secreted you away through Jerndor and brought you to the witch in the woods."

"It sounds like my mother was as bad as the lot of you," he said, his jaw clenched.

"Kethlin approved of sending you away, if that is what you're trying to ask," Nori said. Her face dropped, her biting features saddened at her next words. "She died from complications related to the childbirth before I returned. I wish I could have told her you were safe. She feared you would be killed, that father would do the deed himself. Nobody's allowed to take his throne, not even his children."

"Do you expect me to thank you?" Aleks asked. "Why are you here now? What do you want?"

"It's exactly like before," Nori said. "I know it is. Even if nobody else will admit it. They don't want to see the truth, but I see it."

"See what?" he asked. "Stop being so cryptic."

Nori rolled her eyes and sniffed. "Very well then. I shall state it bluntly. Fritjof. He's back."

Chapter Three: The Forgotten Dragon

"Who?" asked Aleks, confusion darkening his brow. "What are you talking about? Who is Fritjof?"

Nori stared at him aghast. "Fritjof, the dragon," she enunciated slowly as if talking to a toddler. "Does his name ring any bells?"

Aleks shook his head. "I'm afraid not. I never met this Fritjof character."

"But you have heard of him," Nori pressed, standing and pacing. "I know you have. I was there. Remember? You went through his passage; the same one I went through to get to Jerndor."

He followed her with his eyes, exhausted just watching her think. "I remember the passage, but it wasn't named after a dragon. It was named Thief of Peace's Passage to remind fairies how tricky allies could be or something of the sort."

"And?" she pressed, arching an eyebrow.

He shrugged. "Grimkell blames Queen Helena for the Lost Well. It's the only entrance to the fey kingdom other than the passage. The well is supposed to be a source of great power and wealth. Now it's hidden from all of fey because of the Dragomir Treaty. I remember the Lost Well. I was there once, with Hector."

"Do you think you could find it again?"

There was an eager note to her words, and he remembered overhearing Grimkell tell Zaria that the court to control the well ruled the other three. Even here, at the southern tip of Norway, Niffleheim politics reared its ugly head.

Aleks sighed, "I'm not going back there. It's not my home; and not who I want to be."

Nori came to a dead stop. Her voice rose several notches as she said, "That's it? Are you freaking kidding me?" She stopped him with a hand on his shoulder. "Aleks, what do you remember about Koll and his brothers? Surely Hector has told you about them. Dragons are trouble. YOU HAVE TO GO. Fritjof needs to be stopped."

Aleks nodded. "I know all about Koll and his brother, Egil. They're the very worst dragons, the original two —"

"You mean three," Nori interrupted.

"No, I mean two," he said, a thread of annoyance leaking into his voice. He walked over to his closet and pulled down his towel. "Koll's been killed and Egil is locked up again. Everything is good."

"Little brother," she hissed, halting him by the door. "There were three brothers. Fritjof is the third. Somehow he's pulled the memory of his existence from your mind. He's not locked up. He is up to his old tricks."

Aleks crossed his arms and scoffed. "All the dragons wear golden shoes, trapping them in the Under Realm. There's no way he's up to his old tricks even if what you say is true, which it's not. This Fritjof character doesn't exist."

She stormed over and poked him in the chest. "Don't be a fool. Fritjof is the dragon of chaos. He wreaks havoc wherever he goes. He might be physically in the Under Realm now, but he's burrowing his way back into the real world using his old tunnel. If he breaks through it, we're all doomed."

He pushed her finger away and opened the door. The hall lights illuminated her drawn face and tight eyes. "Queen Helena will take care of it. She's the dragon keeper, after all, and a sorceress. You should be talking to her instead of bothering me."

"Queen Helena refuses to take my calls," she said.

"Why is that?" he asked, raising an eyebrow.

She sniffed and tossed her hair. "She said I was delusional. Then she hung up on me."

Aleks barked a laugh. "Perhaps you are."

"I am not delusional, little brother," Nori snarled, looking more like a fox in that moment than he'd ever seen her. It was a good thing his music was loud, or his dad would have heard her.

"Take it easy," Aleks cautioned, pointing through the open door, down the hall. "My father is in the kitchen. My mom is on her way home. Today's been a tough day. Don't cause trouble for me. Just leave."

Nori threw her hands up in the air. "Take your shower, and ignore me then. You're an idiot just like the rest of them. Why did I even come here? You're just as blind as they are. Don't you see Fritjof's influence? Accidents, confusion, disasters, fighting, chaos – it's utter madness out there, and it's only going to get worse."

"Wait, what?" Aleks asked, pausing in the doorway. He turned around and looked her in the eye. "What do you mean?"

"Fritjof is causing infighting with the fairies, starting with the Autumn Court," she said, stepping away from him and drifting further into the bedroom.

"No, I don't care about that," he said, turning from the hallway and shutting the door. "What did you mean by accidents, confusion, disasters? Like a fire at school? An airplane crash? Finding keys in the fridge?"

"What's a fridge?" Nori asked, perplexed. She shook her hand by her head to stop him from replying. "Don't answer that. Are you saying there was a fire and a crash today? Did these things happen to you and your friends?"

"All of that happened to us today," he said. "I thought it was unusual, but unexpected stuff happens. It doesn't always make sense. There's no accounting for plain, old, dumb luck."

"Luck?" Nori repeated scornfully, rolling her eyes. She smacked him on the head. "Idiot. Moron. Numbskull. That was Fritjof trying to target you and your friends."

"Watch it," Aleks warned, stopping her hand from hitting him again. "Older sisters are the worst."

She flashed a half smile at him, a hint of fang peeking out. "I'll take that as a compliment."

"I wouldn't," Aleks said. "I'm glad I didn't have to see you every day growing up."

Nori's eyes narrowed, and her lips thinned. "The feeling is mutual. We need to leave now and get your friends, especially that Zaria girl."

Aleks looked at her suspiciously. When Nori had shown up, he had a feeling it was Zaria she really wanted. "Why do you need Zaria?"

She looked at him like he was pea-brained and made a derisive sniff. "Must I explain everything? While it's almost unbelievable that your friend took down a dragon – and I'm not sure I believe the dwarves, as I'm sure they were trying to pull one over on me – we're going to need her if we plan to stop Fritjof. She at least has some useful magic and can help fight him. It's not like I can talk Fritjof to death."

"There's a thought," Aleks said, smirking at her glare. As much as she got on his nerves, it was only fair he got on hers.

"Fairy magic only goes so far. Even you can't steer him to his doom," Nori said, sighing a little wistfully. "It's such a waste that sorceresses get to do all the truly terrifying spells."

He ignored that remark. "And the others? What do you want with them?"

She gave him a pointed look. "Against all logic, reasonableness, or self-preservation, they seem to come along anyway. It's easier to keep track of them if they're all together from the onset. Get your things. We need to go while your human family is distracted. We've no time to waste."

"It can wait until nightfall," Aleks said, heading back to the hallway. "I'm going to shower and eat with mom and dad. We'll call my friends and prepare them. This way they can gather what they need."

"What do you expect me to do while you dillydally?"

"Sit and read a comic book, play a video game, stare at the ceiling, whatever. I don't care. Just don't be seen. I don't want to have to explain your being here to my parents."

"Very well, if I must wait, I shall," Nori said, sitting gingerly on the bed. "Be quick. Your room makes my skin crawl."

Aleks laughed at her obvious discomfort and shut the door. He whistled as he headed to the bathroom. It was only as he showered that Aleks wondered if it was wise to head on an adventure right now. Could they reach the Under Realm and find Fritjof before his majority? It wasn't in his plans to stay a changeling. He would have to be careful and track the days to ensure he was home before it was too late.

***

Aleks returned to his room after supper to find Nori champing at the bit and raring to go. She yanked him into the room, shut the door with a sharp click, and tossed a backpack at him. He caught it on reflex. It was heavy, filled with who knows what. He slung it over his shoulder.

"I've packed for you, so let's not waste any more time," she said.

"You go ahead. I'm right behind you," he said, hustling her to the window. "I have one more thing to pick up before we go."

"Grab it and be quick, little brother," Nori said, and ducked out.

He watched her walk to the edge of the property. He hurriedly got the stargazer from his shorts, which were on the floor, and stuck it in his pocket. They would need it to keep their parents unaware of their goings-on. He followed out the window, landing in the soft grass. It was nostalgia that made him turn around and carefully shut the window, taking one last, long, look at his safe space, his haven.

"I'll be back in time," he promised, and turned away, catching up with the fiery fairy.

They got Christoffer first. Aleks went to the front door and spoke with his father, Zhuang, while Christoffer said good-bye to his mum and sisters. Their excuse was a sleepover at Filip's.

"At least it's getting easier to sneak away," Christoffer told Aleks, as they walked to the street. "I hate lying, but the truth sounds too farcical for them to believe, and if they believed it, then the truth is that this adventure might be too dangerous, and they wouldn't let me go."

"All kits leave the burrow at some point," Nori said, having overheard the conversation. "Your parents will get over it."

"Hey fox-face," Christoffer said, coolly. "Mind your own business."

Christoffer still held a grudge for being nearly drowned during their underwater competition two years ago. The challenge had turned vicious the moment everyone ducked below the waves. Christoffer had managed to escape by kicking Nori in the chest, but the effort had caused him to be first out of the water, nearly losing the challenge for them. Their last meeting must have run through Nori's mind too, for she flashed her fangs, unable to resist baiting Christoffer, forcing Aleks to separate the two of them before it got ugly.

Geirr was next. His older sister, Kajsa, answered the door. She gave Christoffer a smile and beckoned Aleks and him inside. She looked over their shoulders for a moment, and Aleks hoped Nori was out of sight. He didn't look back to confirm, not wanting to draw further attention her way.

"I'll go get him," Kajsa said, shutting the door and leaving them in the foyer. "He and Torlak are playing some video game or another."

"Is it the new shooter game?" asked Christoffer. "Tell him to bring it."

"Good luck with that," she laughed. "Torlak won't let it out of his sight."

After she disappeared, Aleks raised an inquiring eyebrow. Christoffer shrugged. "What? We're all supposed to be hanging out and having a sleepover at Filip's, right? It matches our story."

"You just want to play the game," Aleks said. "There'll be plenty of time to do that when we're back."

"I can't believe there's another dragon on the loose. I thought we got them all," Christoffer said, leaning against the wall. "Are we certain your sister is right?"

"She's not my sister," Aleks said, before amending, "Not really."

"She is biologically. What am I supposed to call her?"

"I don't know," Aleks said. "I haven't figured that out. Nori, will do."

"Why did she come to you, anyway?" asked Christoffer. "Now that we're away from prying ears we can talk."

"She says Fritjof is one of Koll's brothers and that he's trying to escape into the real world by the same way he used before. Do you remember the passageway we used to get into Jerndor? That's the one. Nori wants Zaria, I think, more than me, but she doesn't know where Zaria lives. I'm the means to an end: we all are, to get Zaria to go with her."

"Did you tell Zaria and Henrik to go to Filip's?" Christoffer asked. "I can text them and tell them to meet us there. This way Nori doesn't learn her location."

"Already done," replied Aleks. "I called her first so they would have enough time to get ready and meet us there."

"Hey guys," Geirr said, coming around the corner. "I'm all set. We should leave before my mom changes her mind. I think she's letting me go tonight because she's hoping more time spent with my friends will mean less time I spend in the sky, flying."

"Haven't you told her yet you plan to open a charter business to fly people around the country?"

Geirr shrugged. "I'll tell her eventually – when it's closer to happening. I certainly wouldn't tell her about it today of all days. Do you think the dragon caused the accident?"

"It's possible," said Aleks. "According to Nori, he's the harbinger of chaos, and everything was normal – until it wasn't – on that landing."

"Too bad crash by dragon interference is not a valid excuse when asked what happened," Geirr said morosely. "I don't know what's worse, knowing what caused the accident or knowing I can't tell people."

They rejoined Nori and made their way to Olaf's bridge. Aleks looked over the rails at the black water below, remembering the first time he'd met the river-troll. It was right after he'd revealed to Zaria that he was a changeling.

It seemed so long ago that Olaf had kidnapped Christoffer to get Zaria in play for the dragon Koll's schemes. That night Olaf had given them a boat and instructed them to find the Hart of Gloomwood Forest. Upon hearing the word "Hart," they assumed he had meant "heart" and they had gone north in search of this "heart" not knowing that the Hart in question was neither the center of the forest, the heart of a tree within the forest, nor a heart-shaped necklace found on a stag within a golden glade in the midst of the forest. Hart was the stag himself, which bore the heart-shaped necklace and was the future of the ellefolken people.

Trading Hart for the freedom of their friend Christoffer had had many rolling consequences; the first was that the loss of Hart impeded his father, Hector, from taking his rightful place within the golden circle of Gloomwood Forest. Hector could not transform into a Golden King if his son was not free to also transform and take the mantle of Stag Lord from him.

If the male royal line could not transform to strengthen their guardianship of the Under Realm, the dragons could rot the golden trees and break through their line of defense, thus escaping from their prison void into the real world, where they would cause unimaginable pain and suffering.

Together they had saved Hart, freeing Hector and Hart to transform into their new forms, and Koll had been defeated, destroyed by Zaria's magic for good, never to return, and his brother Egil had been recaptured.

The troll had been under the influence of Koll, who'd been desperate to reclaim his old territory. Left without a guardian, the Gjöll River protected the Under Realm with wild magic. Now that Olaf was back in his right mind, he remembered the reasons he had given up guardianship of the river and was ashamed of his past actions. Tonight, they weren't rescuing anyone, but they were once again heading north into the unknown, to fight off a dragon's attempt to upend the world.

If Nori was right, then they had missed Fritjof in the chaos of the battle two years ago. If they had, he must be roaming loose in the Under Realm, seeking as dragons would, with unparalleled determination for a way out of the prison's boundaries. Would they capture him before his escape? If they did, then what?

Aleks wondered just how many dragons there were in the Under Realm. He knew of four, well five, if you counted Koll, who was now dead. The others were Koll's younger brothers, Egil and Fritjof, and the twin dragons of war. Aleks didn't know much about the last two, as Queen Helena had mentioned them briefly and only to Zaria.

Filip's home was a short distance from the bridge. They saw light spilling from his upstairs bedroom window. Aleks and Christoffer went around the side of the building, where Christoffer picked up a rock and tossed it next to the window. It bounced off the side of the house, and Filip, clearly waiting for them, stuck out his head.

"Are Zaria and Henrik with you?" Aleks asked.

"We got here just a few minutes ago," Zaria said, sticking her head out the window next to Filip's. She waved. "Come on up!"

"Send Henrik down to talk with Nori," Aleks said, flashing the stargazer at her before hiding it in his pocket.

"Its magic doesn't affect Zaria," Christoffer said, looking at it. "She's a sorceress. They should both come down."

"We'll keep Nori distracted," Zaria promised.

"I'll be right down, too," said Filip, hands braced on the windowsill. "This way everyone won't have to come up here."

He shut the window and disappeared. Aleks and Christoffer headed around to the front of the house. As they approached, Geirr rang the doorbell.

When Mrs. Storstrand answered, Zaria and Henrik were already at the bottom of the stairs with their bags slung over their shoulders. Filip's mum looked askance at them.

"We'll be right back, Mrs. Storstrand," Zaria said cheerfully. "I forgot something at the house and Henrik is escorting me so I'm not alone. I'm sorry for the inconvenience."

"It's fine," she said as they slipped out around her into the dark. "It's getting late. I don't want you two walking back on your own. If your father can't drop you off again, call Filip. I'll come get you."

"Thank you," Henrik said, ever polite. "That's very kind of you."

Mrs. Storstrand smiled warmly at him. She was a woman in her mid-forties with classic Nordic coloring. She was a little on the plump side, giving her a charming and warm appearance. She always welcomed Aleks with a smile and some sort of sweets. Mrs. Storstrand was an excellent baker and she liked to make them desserts when they came over. His favorite was her walnut shortbread cookies.

Aleks lost sight of them when the door shut. Waving good-bye to Mrs. Storstrand, the three went up the stairs, meeting Filip at the top. He not only had his backpack all ready, but also had an extra by his feet.

Geirr poked it with his foot. "Why do you have two bags? What's in the second?"

Filip shrugged. "In case the first one is lost again. I'd rather have to carry two backpacks than go without like before. I missed my stuff!"

"You have no sense of adventure," Christoffer grumbled good-naturedly. "When else are we going to be able to go for days without showering or washing our clothes?"

Filip's cheeks reddened slightly. "I don't want to worry about body odor. It's not a crime."

"You crush on her so hard," Christoffer teased, referring to Zaria. "Why don't you just tell her?"

"Shut up," Filip said, kicking the backpack by his feet at Christoffer, who just barely caught it. "Shouldn't we use the stargazer? Let's go."

Aleks and Geirr exchanged looks, but wisely kept silent. Filip was sensitive about his feelings for Zaria. Now was not the time to rile him up, especially when she was right outside.

Aleks took the stargazer out of his pocket. The boys all linked arms, but left Aleks with a free hand. He pressed the insert on the largest star. Nothing visible showed that the stargazer activated. No warbles in space or light to indicate magic had happened.

"This was so anticlimactic compared to last time," Geirr said, dropping his arms. "Your mum isn't chasing after us, trying to get you to come home."

Filip ran a hand through his hair. "I took so much heat for that when we got back. She still mutters to this day, two years later, that I wasn't punished nearly long enough. You and I know that I never was punished, but she doesn't know that."

"How's your brother doing anyway?" asked Geirr. "Is he liking Uni?"

Filip shrugged. "I guess so, we don't really talk much while he's gone. It's too hard to keep up with our different schedules. That's why mum is so insistent on us having family time when he's back. He's got less than a year left, and then he has to decide whether he wants a master's or to go to work."

He hugged his mum as they walked past her frozen figure. She was staring up the stairs as if she was trying to get a good look at them. Aleks waited as Filip shut and locked the door behind them, putting his keys into his backpack.

Nori glowered at them. "Do you think we aren't in a hurry? We have to go. Now."

"Is she going to be like this the whole time?" Geirr asked, sharing a sidelong look with him.

"I hope not," Aleks said darkly, his response making Geirr laugh.

Nori got on everyone's nerves. Even Henrik, who was by far the most even-tempered of them all, began to show signs of snapping. They hadn't even gotten out of the city yet, and already Aleks wanted to strangle her. If she sniffed one more time, he wouldn't be responsible for what he did next.

She complained about everything. First it was the smell of garbage and pollution, then the state of the streets, next the buildings were too tall, the trees too few, the lights too bright, and on, and on, and on. She hadn't one nice thing to say about Fredrikstad or humans. If all fairies were like her, Aleks fully understood why they were cut off from their well and the world. The dwarf that let her out of Niffleheim had some serious explaining to do.

Chapter Four: A Bear of a Time

"Why are we helping her again?" Geirr asked under his breath, giving Aleks a sidelong glance.

He sighed. "Because whether I like it or not, she made her point about this dragon. Too many weird things happened in such a short span of time to discount it all as coincidence."

"If she doesn't shut up, I won't be held accountable for my actions," Christoffer hissed to them, echoing Aleks' earlier thoughts.

"I won't stop you," he told his friend.

"I'll join you," said Geirr, causing all three to chuckle.

"Humans think they're so clever," Nori remarked as they passed a library. "They forget more things than they learn. A place to store knowledge is wasted on them —"

"Enough," Zaria said, cutting her off. "Take some human advice. If you can't say something nice, don't say anything at all."

Leave it to a bookworm to get her dander up about a library, Aleks mused. He grinned at Zaria, giving her a thumbs-up. Affronted, Nori stormed ahead of them. He was grateful. If Zaria hadn't said something, Nori would have kept on prattling.

"Thank God," Filip said with evident relief. He looked to Aleks. "She's not good for the dynamics of this adventure, mate. She's trouble with a capital T. You know I'm right."

Henrik, who was back in his traditional ellefolken clothing, wore a white pelt cloak with golden antlers. The cloak made soft swishing sounds as he walked. The antlers cast branch-like shadows on the ground ahead of them. He glanced meaningfully at Nori.

"I agree," he said. "Her temperament is not conducive to this quest. It's actually very harmful."

"I could cause her bodily harm," Geirr muttered, when she sniffed derisively and flounced again.

Henrik cracked a smile and offered, "I could sneak up on her and stash her somewhere." Zaria frowned at them. Aleks shook his head. He shrugged, stuffing his hands into his pants' pockets. "It was only a suggestion," he said lightly.

"The best one I've heard tonight," Christoffer said, clapping him on the back. "Now, are we going to walk the entire way to Niffleheim? That's going to take ages and ages. We could all use a winter-wyvern right about now."

A sharp, short whistle from Henrik startled the group. As one, they looked to him. He tipped his chin to the sky. "I called Norwick," he explained.

Nori glared at him. "I have transportation for us. Call off your beast."

He did, sending out another sharp whistle with a different series of notes. "Done," Henrik said.

"How come he listens to you?" asked Geirr, puzzled. "Wasn't he Hector's wyvern?"

"Now that my father is a Golden King, Norwick belongs to me," said Henrik. "In fact all his stuff does. I'm still sorting through some of it. He kept a lot of journals."

"He did?" asked Zaria, her eyes growing bigger. "Can I read them? What are they about?"

A half-grin tugged on Henrik's mouth. "You can read them. I don't think he'd mind. He left me a lot of notes on his trades – the people, what he traded, good deals, worse deals, trade routes, etc. He shares stories about my mother before she –"

Zaria gasped. "She's not dead is she?"

Henrik rushed to assure her. "She's with Hector."

"In the Under Realm?" Zaria asked, surprised.

He shook his head. "No. She transformed above on the surface, to be closer to him. She and my father communicate through Hakon."

"Was it a great romance?" Zaria asked, practically gushing. Beside him Filip cursed under his breath.

Hector, Henrik's father, wasn't dead as Zaria's last words implied. He was simply a tree – an alder tree specifically, with a golden trunk and branches, and pure white leaves. Aleks had been present when Hector became the reigning Golden King, taking over the mantle of his father, Hakon, and saving the Golden Kings from the corrosive and corruptive rot spread by the dragons.

The ellefolken are able to change into elk, human, or tree forms. The females can transform multiple times, taking whichever shape pleases them, switching back and forth at will. The males, however, can transform only once, starting life as an elk, transforming to a human, then to a tree. They can never change back once they progress into the new form.

When in the elk form, the males are known as Hart. This had been the source of confusion when they had attempted to rescue Christoffer back at the very beginning. Olaf had been wickedly amused knowing that they hadn't a clue what they'd been willing to trade in exchange for their friend. Now when a troll offered a deal, they knew better than to take anything at face value. Rescuing Hart had been a series of challenges all its own.

In his human form, Hart, their friend, and also past and future Harts, took a name of their choosing and the title Stag Lord as an official prince of Elleken, the wandering seat of the ellefolken. Aleks and the others hadn't had a chance to visit it yet, but Henrik had promised to take them someday.

The last transformation was into an alder tree. The newest tree becomes the ruling king, but he also becomes one of many Golden Kings. Together the kings' roots anchor the Under Realm to the real world, forming an impenetrable barrier that dragons can't sneak past.

The ellefolken are naturally rot resistant, which makes their roots the perfect set of bars for a prison holding dragons. That resistance, though, doesn't mean that they are infallible. As the group saw last time, almost the whole circle of kings had rotted under the dragons' pernicious influences.

When Hector had taken his place amongst the Golden Kings, he had done so within the Under Realm, effectively cutting himself off from his people. Getting into the Under Realm isn't an easy thing to do. One required a special pair of shoes with Queen Helena's magical signature locking them into place. Then to leave, it required that she or Zaria remove the invisible magical lock on the shoes.

Queen Helena had promised to allow Henrik entrance as often as he needed it to speak with his father, but apparently hadn't extended the offer to Henrik's mother. For Henrik, summer would've been ideal for visitation, since he was a student with them; but Hector had promised the witch in the woods that Henrik would spend five summers helping her in exchange for the pairs of golden shoes they had needed to get across the Gjallarbrú, a bridge that spanned the Gjöll. One summer for each pair.

"Have you visited your dad recently?" asked Aleks, as he refocused on the group. Nori was almost out of eyesight. He picked up his pace.

Henrik shook his head. "Not since before the summer started. Working for the witch doesn't leave me much time or energy. It's labor intensive. She's had me chopping wood, rearranging furniture, purchasing furniture from Petronella the Measureless, plowing fields, and sorting stones."

Petronella was the giantess ruler of the tribe living on the Varanger Peninsula in Jötunheim. Other than Henrik, nobody in the group had met her officially.

Christoffer raised a hand. "What do you mean sorting stones?"

Henrik made hand motions. "I move stones from one pile to another. Some days she wants them sorted by weight. Other days she wants them sorted by size. Some days I even organize by their color. Whichever way she wants me to organize, I do it."

"Do you mean gem stones?" Zaria asked, her eyebrows knitting together.

"No," Henrik chuckled. "I wish. I mean boulders. I don't understand half the things she wants me to do, but I do them."

"I feel badly that you're on your own," Christoffer said. "It doesn't seem right that you're paying for all of our shoes."

Henrik waved his concern away. "It's what my father and king wanted. It's a small price to pay to save the Golden Kings and the Under Realm from destruction."

When he said things like that, Henrik didn't seem like a sixteen year old to Aleks. Ellefolken live a long time, so who knew exactly how old Henrik was. Outwardly he appeared to be their age, so nobody questioned him about it. Only his speech sometimes gave away that he wasn't the normal teen he looked like. He'd been taught by generations of his forefathers about the world that he would move in – magical and non-magical aspects alike. This explained why he sometimes sounded older than he looked.

Aleks hurried them along, and the group caught up to Nori at the outskirts of town. He spotted her as she leaned against a tree, arms crossed, thrumming her fingers impatiently. Seeing them, she flicked her hair behind her shoulder and straightened.

"It's a wonder that you accomplish anything," she said by way of greeting. "A whole horde of baby trolls could round you up without breaking a sweat. You're too loud and too slow."

"Ease up, Nori," Aleks said. "You're not in charge."

"And you are?" she challenged, bristling. "This should be fun. I can't wait to see you fall flat on your face, baby brother. What is your plan? We might as well give up right now."

He glared at her. "Where are we going, and how are we getting there?"

Nori rubbed the bridge of her nose, as if she found him trying her patience already. "Where else are we going, but to Niffleheim? The quickest route is to the Lost Well. This is where you come in."

"No," said Aleks. "We're not showing you its location. It's going to stay lost."

She pulled a face. "Fine. We'll return the way I came. We'll find the Trolgar mirror, take it into Jerndor, transfer to the Thief of Peace's tunnel, and finally arrive home, whatever may be left of it."

Aleks stopped walking, causing Christoffer to collide with him. "Niffleheim is not home. Wouldn't it be better to seek out Queen Helena and the Under Realm? Isn't that where Fritjof is now?"

"I told you," Nori said, exasperated. "Queen Helena won't return my overtures."

"She'd return Zaria's," Henrik said, patting his backpack. "I've got the mirror. You could have a word with her."

Zaria rubbed the back of her neck, hesitating. "What am I going to tell her? No offense, but Nori hasn't exactly provided proof, and today's events are a bit circumstantial at best."

"Are you calling me a liar?" Nori asked, her red hair practically bristling.

Zaria shook her head. "I'm not saying that, either. I just want to wait. I don't want to involve her unless I have to. Our relationship is still so new."

"It's been two years, Zaria. What could it hurt?" Aleks countered. "It could save us a trip." At his nod, Henrik pulled out the mirror.

She sighed and took it, walking a little ways off into the woods. Filip hovered near the group of trees she'd disappeared amid, looking like he wanted to follow her. Aleks crossed his arms and leaned against a nearby tree.

Nori affected a casual stance, but as relaxed as she looked, Aleks knew she was poised to spring into action. She watched the spot where Zaria would return with beady-eyed intensity.

"We should light up some lanterns now that we're outside the city," said Henrik, pulling one out of his bag. He turned it on, illuminating the area in a steady man-made glow.

Aleks found his lantern and turned it on, brightening the circle around them. Geirr needed to snag a set of batteries for his, but soon had it illuminated. Zaria reappeared with a worried look on her face, as the last lantern was lit. She held the mirror loosely at her side, her fingers tapping the surface nervously.

"Any luck?" asked Filip.

She shook her head and gave the mirror to Henrik. "As soon as I mentioned Fritjof's name, she hung up on me. I called her back, and she claimed interference, so I repeated the question, but the call cut off again.

"I got worried so I called Ava to test the connection. We spoke briefly, I said I was having trouble reaching my birth mother. We hung up, and I tried Helena again, but the mirror won't dial her anymore."

"That sucks. Do you think it's Helena blocking you? Or is it something else?" asked Christoffer.

"Could Fritjof block an enchanted device?" Aleks asked, looking between Henrik and Nori.

Henrik's brow furrowed. "From within the Under Realm? I don't see how."

"Of course he could. This is Fritjof we're talking about," Nori huffed. Her tone stated clearly that she thought the new Stag Lord was an idiot.

Henrik glowered at her. "Even my father can't communicate to us up here, and he's part of the border guard. He has to relay his message through his predecessors who are topside."

"A Golden King is not a dragon," Nori said with a little sniff. "Now can we please keep moving? We're almost there."

"Where's that?" Zaria asked.

"Where I tied up our beasts of burden," Nori said. "We'll get to Trolgar a lot faster on them than if we went by foot."

"Winter-wyverns?" Christoffer asked hopefully. He'd finally had a chance to ride one on the return trip from the Under Realm and had been thrilled about it ever since, wanting to go up in the air again.

Nori sighed like a longsuffering mother. "The fey live in an underground void. Why would I have access to winter-wyverns? We'll be riding on bears."

"No winter-wyverns, but you have bears? How does that make sense?" Christoffer complained, and then, in an aside to Aleks, he added, "I'm surprised the bears didn't eat her."

Aleks snorted, quickly suppressing laughter, as Nori turned a scowl at them. "They're too smart for that," he said.

"Hah," Christoffer agreed. "They probably know she'd give them indigestion."

The group came across the bears about an hour later. There were four of them, which meant Aleks and his friends would have to double up. He was just grateful there weren't three bears. In that scenario he knew his friends would make him ride with Nori. The thought gave him hives. At least with four bears, she could ride alone.

The bears were tied up to the trunks of different trees. A white bear on his hind legs stretched his body and braced against a tree. Right above him was a bees' nest, a massive, lopsided, lump sitting precariously on a branch.

The other bears were smaller, brown bears with a range of colored pelts. They were industriously munching in the bushes getting their fill of berries, their heads so far inside that he couldn't see them. The bears grunted as the lanterns flooded the clearing in light.

Nori walked over to some dense bushes that were outside of the bears' range and pulled out saddles, reins, armor, bags, and canteens. Henrik went to examine the lone polar bear. He spoke soothingly to the creature, as Aleks and the others watched. Then he braced a foot on the bear's back and climbed over it and up the tree to the hive.

"He's crazy," Filip said. "He's going to get stung."

"Are bees active at night? Do polar bears even like honey?" Christoffer asked, joining them and watching their friend use a knife to cut the hive loose.

"Watch out," Henrik shouted as part of the hive broke off and fell down.

Zaria, who'd been helping Nori untangle the reins, turned around. She squinted, and Aleks knew she was performing magic. She didn't need to squint, but sometimes even now she couldn't help making the expression or twitching her hands. It was almost an ingrained habit.

Any outward sign of her magic was simply for show, for Zaria's magic didn't come from hand gestures or words, like most sorceresses. Her magic came from her thoughts, but that was supposed to be a secret, hence squinty eyes and twitchy hands. If the dragons found out the true nature of her gifts, she'd be in serious trouble.

The hive stopped an inch from hitting the ground and breaking open. Bees buzzed, flying out of it with an angry hum. Zaria let it drop, and it thudded gently down. A strong breeze blew the bees away from the area – another of Zaria's tricks.

Henrik looked down sheepishly from his perch in the tree. "Sorry," he said. "I thought the honey would be good for the bear and for us to have."

The bear was indeed happy with the honey. It snuffled the intact hive and started to break it apart with its teeth. Henrik jumped down and tucked the other half of the hive into a plastic bag and then into his main bag.

"Don't let it eat that," Nori scolded. "Polar bears need lots of meat and fat. I brought it food."

She pulled a wrapped package of raw meat from one of the saddlebags. After taking off the paper, she tossed it to the bear. Its attention turned at once from the beehive to the meat, allowing Henrik to deftly swipe the hive and hide it in his bag. The meat was gone in a flash.

Nori sniffed approvingly and patted the bear's neck. "Now if you're through delaying us Stag Lord, let's saddle up and get away from here."

Aleks and Filip struggled to put the saddle and harness on their bear, but it kept side-stepping just as the saddle was lowered, or moved into them and knocked them over. Filip cursed as he landed on his backside for the second time in as many minutes. Aleks laughed and offered a hand up.

"How do we get this thing on it?" Filip asked, crossing his arms and glaring at the beast.

Aleks watched Henrik effortlessly swing the heavy saddle up and onto his bear's back. The kid had serious muscles from moving those boulders during his summer with the witch. Geirr threaded the reins through the harness and joined him.

Nori was already mounted on her bear. She glared at him when their eyes met. Aleks made a face and focused on Christoffer and Zaria. That was no use either, as after some arguing with Christoffer, Zaria used her magic. With a wave of her hand, she lifted the saddle onto the bear and secured it in place.

Zaria was gaining more control, but using magic wasn't her first instinct. When Christoffer had questioned her about it in the past, she'd shrugged and said that doing things on her own was as rewarding as magic. Christoffer thought that was nuts, and at the time Aleks had agreed with him outwardly. Privately, he'd agreed with Zaria. To rely on himself, rather than magic, was one of the main reasons he wanted to become human.

"No help for it," Aleks said with a sigh. "We just have to try again."

"Ugh," said Filip with feeling. "Fine. Let's do this."

They grabbed the saddle and lifted it, grunting with the effort. With a quick side step they hurled it over the bear's back. It landed heavily, much to the bear's protest, and nearly slipped off. Aleks grabbed the edge as it tipped precariously to the side. They hauled it back in place. Filip wiped his hands with satisfaction.

"You secure it under its belly. I'll grab the harness," said Aleks.

Filip nodded and squatted, reaching low under the bear to find the straps. Aleks took the reins and harness over to the bear's head. It snorted in his face, blowing his hair back. The beast had terrible breath. Aleks wrinkled his nose in disgust.

The bear fought his attempts to put on its harness, tossing its head this way and that, nearly crushing Filip in the process. Filip rolled a safe distance away from the bear's stomping feet.

"Honestly," Nori growled, sliding off her bear.

She marched over, snatched the reins from Aleks, and wrestled the bear into submission. In less than a minute the harness was in place and the reins were wrapped loosely around the saddle horn. She tightened and buckled the saddle, slapping her thighs as she stood.

"You two are incompetent," she sneered. "Do you think you can manage getting on the creature or should I help you with that, too?"

Chapter Five: The Horn
of the Dilemma

"Thanks, but we've got it," Aleks said roughly, pushing her aside. "Come on, Filip."

He and Filip swung onto the bear's back. Aleks grabbed the reins and steered the creature around to join the others. Nori moved her bear to the front of the pack, taking the lead. She sat erect with a stately air about her, looking every inch like a noble. Her long, red hair swayed gently as she moved. She was poised and confident as she navigated the woods.

After some time, in the dead of night, when everyone's stomachs began to growl incessantly, Zaria directed her and Christoffer's bear closer to the others. She conjured up some sandwiches and handed them each one. Filip tore into his like a starving man.

"Can I have another?" he asked between mouthfuls. "With Swiss cheese this time?"

Zaria laughed gaily and another sandwich appeared in her hand. Filip took it with a nod of thanks, before polishing off the one he was eating. She and Christoffer moved away to offer Henrik and Geirr some of the same.

"Chew with your mouth closed," Aleks said, elbowing him. "It's disgusting to hear you chew."

Filip swallowed noisily and whispered loudly, "Am I really that bad? Do you think Zaria noticed?"

Aleks grinned. "Hard not to hear you, man. You're loud enough to drown out conversation."

Filip groaned. "Kill me now."

"It's more fun to watch you squirm. Relax, I'm joking. She didn't hear you."

Filip shoved him. "Some friend you are, scaring me like that."

"Hey, Zaria!" Aleks called. "Filip has —"

Filip's hand clapped over his mouth, so the rest of his sentence came out muffled. Zaria looked back and smiled. Filip waved as if to say, "Nothing to see here."

Aleks broke away, taking a deep breath as if to try again, and Filip tackled him. They fell off their bear and struggled in the dirt. He laughed mightily at his friend's furious attempts to silence him. Aleks wasn't going to say anything, but Filip didn't know that.

"Idiots," Nori muttered. She looked at Zaria. "I don't know how you stand them."

Zaria shrugged. "They're my friends."

Nori harrumphed. "Stop fighting," she commanded. "We're here."

Filip stopped trying to punch him into submission. Aleks shoved him off and sat up with Christoffer's help. Something wasn't quite right, but Aleks couldn't put his finger on it. He looked around the clearing trying to figure it out.

"Hey, mate," Filip said casually, as if he hadn't just been trying to beat Aleks up. "Isn't it odd to you that we reached Trolgar so quickly? It took us longer by boat than it did by bear."

Aleks frowned, thinking. The memory was foggy in his mind, but yes, the vague uneasy feeling he had was the fact that it should have taken longer. Either he was wrong or Nori was.

"Nori," he began slowly, turning around to find her. "Where is here?"

"Trolgar," she stated with a haughty hair flip.

"We should have at least another full day of travel," Henrik said, looking concerned. "Shouldn't we?" He rubbed his forehead as if to clear his thoughts.

"This is Trolgar," Nori insisted. "I would know. Didn't I just have to come through here to find you?"

"Are the bears enhanced with magic?" Henrik asked, handing the reins to Geirr and sliding off.

Nori frowned. "No. Where would you get a ridiculous idea like that?"

"Because Nori," Aleks said, waving a hand at their surroundings, "we haven't traveled long enough to get to Trolgar, unless the bears were magical and could travel far in a short amount of time."

"This again?" Nori asked. She hopped down and marched toward the biggest tree. "The mirror for Jerndor from Trolgar is right…" she hesitated, looking around confused. "Here."

"I don't see anything," Christoffer said. "I think your sister is nuts."

"She's not my sister," Aleks said absently, moving toward where Nori stood.

"He's said that before," Christoffer muttered to Zaria, not quite low enough to escape Aleks' hearing.

"Shh," Zaria said, hushing him. "Leave it alone."

"They *are* related," Christoffer whined, pouting at Zaria's vehement glare.

Aleks ignored them and focused his attention on Nori, who looked to be panicking. She kept moving from tree to tree trying to find the hidden mirror. Her cool façade cracked as she completed the circle. She clutched at her throat, her eyes glazed over, and she mumbled something to herself. Aleks approached slowly, hands out.

"It's okay," he told her.

"No, it's not," Nori shot back. "I'm all confused. This should be the spot. This is Trolgar. I know it. I know it."

He made his voice as soothing as possible. "Nori, you can see that it's not. We still have a ways to go."

She bobbed her head. "Right. That's it of course, we just stopped too soon. Everyone get back on your bears," she commanded, grasping at her saddle.

"We should camp for the night. Start fresh in the morning," Henrik said.

"No, we have to hurry," Nori said. "We're short on time as it is. We can't get delayed."

Nori mounted her bear swiftly and kicked it into motion. She took off like a shot leaving them behind. Aleks shared a worried look with Zaria and Henrik.

"We can't let her go off alone. Something isn't right with her," Zaria said from her perch on her bear. She had never climbed down.

Aleks nodded, and he and Filip clambered onto their bear. Henrik got on his, and Christoffer got behind Zaria again. At his signal, they kicked their bears into motion, chasing after Nori. Aleks located her by sound and urged his bear in her direction. After a few intense minutes of riding at full speed, he spied her in the trees ahead.

Nori swerved chaotically around trees, leading them on a merry dance. Aleks tried to catch up to her. He and the others even shouted at her to stop, but she didn't hear or didn't heed them, if she did. Soon Nori outstripped them again. All they could see of her was a white speck moving like a ghost in the dark forest. Then she was gone completely out of sight.

"That polar bear can move," Geirr said as Henrik called for a halt.

"No kidding," Christoffer replied, his voice slightly hoarse from yelling at the fairy to stop. He took a deep drink of water from a canteen, backhanding his lips when he was done. He passed it to Zaria who drank greedily.

"What now?" Aleks asked as they slowed down, letting their winded bears catch their breaths.

"We know where she's trying to go. Let's head there," Zaria suggested. She was a bit worse for wear from the ride and took the time to straighten up and fix her hair.

"Zar-Zar is right," said Filip. "She wants to get to Niffleheim, and her path there is through Trolgar and Jerndor. We can catch up with her along the way."

"The bears will need some rest after that run," Henrik said, rubbing the ears of his beast. "I wonder what got into her."

Aleks shrugged. "I don't know, but I'm not going to lie and say I'm sorry she's gone."

"She opens her mouth, and my skin crawls," Christoffer said, shuddering for effect.

"That's just her natural appeal coming through," Geirr joked. "If it's all right with everyone, I'm going to go stretch my legs. I'm stiff as a board."

Henrik nodded and began checking all the saddle bags Nori had left them. Christoffer helped, and together the two took inventory. Most of the bags held wrapped food for the bears, but there were also some heavy-duty flashlights, batteries, a ball of twine, and other odds and ends.

"It's a good thing we packed our own food," Christoffer said when they were done. "If we hadn't, we'd be rationing."

Henrik nodded. "She brought just enough to feed the bears and maybe herself."

Aleks grunted. "Figures. She wasn't thinking clearly on the trip down."

"Or on the return trip," Geirr added, rejoining the group. "It's a good thing that Zaria's with us, because I didn't pack a lot of food either."

"Oh great," Zaria said with a laugh. "Did I just become the glorified cook on this trip?"

Christoffer slung an arm around her neck. "Zaria, Zaria, it's not like that –"

"Even though it is," Aleks said, smirking.

"Aleks, shut it," Christoffer fake whispered. "You'll upset her, and then she won't feed us."

Zaria laughed and elbowed him in the ribs. "I just might not feed *you*, you great lummox."

"Look what you've done," Christoffer said, continuing to whisper. "She's breaking out the big words now."

Zaria stuck out her tongue at him. They dissolved into giggles. It was the wee hours of the morning, and nobody felt like continuing. They camped in a ring, sticking close to the bears for warmth after they decided to not light a fire. It had been an exhausting day for them all, with one strange thing happening after another. Aleks didn't know about the others, but he slept like a rock.

In the morning, after a breakfast of granola and fruit, augmented by a few magical dishes from Zaria, they took down their makeshift camp. As Aleks rolled up his sleeping bag, he suppressed a grin at Filip's flaming face as he assisted Zaria with hers. He then cast a quick glance at Henrik standing solemnly beside his own bear. Aleks couldn't figure out his expression. Was it wistful? Was it indifference? He couldn't tell.

"We've got plenty of daylight," Henrik said, glancing to the sky where sunlight dappled through the trees. It was well past dawn. "We should use it and not linger."

"I'm saddle sore," Geirr said. "Can't I walk for a bit?"

Henrik gave his consent, but added, "Not for long, though. We mustn't let Nori get so far ahead of us that she's left Trolgar and entered Jerndor."

"Who's to say she'll wait for us even there?" asked Zaria. "She's too wound up to stay in one place for long. She's desperate to get back to Niffleheim."

"We'll just have to hope that she does," said Henrik.

"I hope she doesn't," whispered Christoffer in an aside to Aleks.

He nodded and finished repacking the last of the saddlebags. Then he strapped his backpack to the bear and climbed onto the saddle. Geirr groaned, taking a few more minutes to stretch his legs, but he, too, eventually got back on his and Henrik's bear and the group was off.

Christoffer nattered incessantly in his ear. Aleks listened as he talked about the weather, the fact that they were riding bears, his plans for Zaria's magical feasts at lunch – and dinnertime, his annoyance at Nori, and his speculation about Filip and Zaria. In short, it was a long day on bear-back, without much excitement.

"They look cozy, don't they?" Christoffer noted, as the sun began to set.

Aleks watched them. Filip looked a lot more relaxed after a day spent casually pointing out wildlife to Zaria and touching her arms and waist. They both looked happy, but Aleks didn't know and couldn't guess at Zaria's internal thoughts.

Did she see Filip as a friend or as possibly something more? He knew Filip would be devastated if she rejected him. He could only hope his friend's feelings weren't misplaced.

"We're almost to Trolgar," Henrik said as everyone dismounted for the night. "No more than half a day's journey lies ahead of us. Zaria, you should try reaching Queen Helena again. The guys and I will set up camp for this evening."

She nodded, taking the mirror from Henrik and settling against a tree. Aleks and Filip went to gather wood, as Christoffer and Geirr set up tents and Henrik fed the bears before heading into the woods to set up snares and booby-traps. Aleks waited until they were away from camp and couldn't be overheard before he brought up Filip's crush.

"Did you have a nice ride this afternoon with Zaria?" he asked.

"Shh," Filip said, shushing him. A wide grin split his face in two.

Aleks gave an answering one in return. "That good, huh? It looked like you were enjoying yourself."

"Come on, mate, keep your voice down, she could hear you." Filip looked nervously over his shoulder.

"Relax," Aleks said, chuckling. "She can't hear us."

"Thanks for arranging that," Filip said, after confirming that Zaria was nowhere in sight. "It was nice to ride with her."

"More than nice," Aleks teased. "You were beet red for a while."

Filip blushed again and bent to gather some broken sticks to hide it. "I like her a lot, okay?" he said, glancing up.

"Trust me, we know," Aleks said, then asked, "Does she?"

"I haven't told her yet," Filip admitted.

Aleks stacked his armful of wood on top of Filip's pile. "You should. Don't wait, man."

"Every time I see her I get tied up in knots," Filip said, following Aleks as he continued to pick up firewood. "I'm afraid of looking like a fool."

"You are a fool," Aleks said helpfully.

"Do you think I'm friend-zoned?" Filip asked, looking worried. "What if she says she's not interested? I wouldn't be able to face her. Maybe I should tell her after we take care of this new dragon. Then if she rejects me, I can wallow in privacy."

Aleks listened patiently as Filip documented his woes. Finally he said, "Look, do us all a favor. Ask her. Then you'll know. You'll feel better, and the rest of us won't have to keep it a secret anymore."

Filip followed him back to the camp, lost in thought. As they got closer, a shadow flickered in the trees. Turning his head abruptly, Aleks stopped walking to stare in the direction of the movement. Filip ran into him dropping half his pile. He scrambled to pick it all up, but Aleks stopped him.

"Do you see anything?" he asked, nodding toward the trees.

Filip squinted. "Trees."

Aleks kicked him. "Something in the trees, pinhead."

Filip looked again, and so did he. Whatever it was, though, was gone. Aleks didn't like it. The shadow hadn't felt like an animal. It couldn't be Nori, could it? He didn't think she'd double-back to fetch them – not in the hurry she'd been in to reach Trolgar. And why would she hide?

"Let's get back to camp," Aleks said, keeping a wary eye on the spot.

The two returned without incident. Henrik was just finishing tying up the bears to some trees using a long rope Nori had supplied. Zaria was sitting with Geirr on a blanket conjuring up dishes. She was creating a smorgasbord. There were several small fish dishes like pickled herring and dill-cured salmon, beetroot salad, apple salad, cold meats, mini meatballs, breads, and cheeses. The sight had Aleks salivating, and dessert, he prayed, would be apple cake, his favorite.

"Did you finish setting up the snares and traps?" Aleks asked Henrik.

"I did," Henrik said. "I used a couple of my father's favorite traps. This close to troll country, we'd be wise to use them. Keep them at bay."

Aleks tilted his head in the direction they'd come from. "I saw movement out in the woods."

"Trolls?" Geirr asked, already making himself a plate. "Do you think we're all still on the same side?"

Henrik said jovially, "Trolls are always on their side. Are you certain it wasn't Nori or Norwick?"

"You called him off," Zaria reminded him.

Henrik frowned. "So I did. He might have come on his own anyway, though. He's quite independent."

"No fog," Aleks said as he and Filip dropped their armfuls of wood and started making a fire.

"Were you able to reach Helena?" Filip asked Zaria, as he retrieved matches from one of his backpacks.

Zaria shot Henrik a worried look before turning back and saying, "She didn't answer. I think the mirror is no longer able to reach her at all."

"That's not good," said Filip. He rubbed his jaw, thinking. "Don't you have another way to reach her, Henrik? Didn't she have something like a horn in the Under Realm? She used it to communicate with Silje before we came to the real world."

Henrik went to his bag and took out a horn matching the one Filip described. "Do you mean this? The Gjallarhorn?"

Filip nodded. "That's it. Did she have one like that?"

Henrik turned the horn over in his hands, thinking. "I'm almost certain she does. Most leaders do."

He put the horn to his lips and blew. A high-pitched velvety sound drifted out and winged through the air. The sound of the horn faded, and Henrik pulled it away from his lips, peering into it. He tapped the horn against his hand and brought it up again. Another short call danced in the air, before its song drifted away.

"Either she's not answering, or this is broken," Henrik said, looking at them with a worried frown. He blew again and Silje, the queen of the elves, appeared like a ghostly hologram before them, all her brilliant coloring missing.

"Hello, Queen Silje," Henrik said formally, offering a little bow.

She nodded to him. "Yes, Stag Lord? How may I help you?"

"I am trying to contact Queen Helena about some intelligence I've received from the fey courts. Have you had difficulties reaching her?"

Silje tilted her head and tapped a finger to her chin. "We last spoke a week ago. What intelligence have you received, and from the fey courts no less? I didn't think we were on speaking terms with them."

Henrik rubbed the back of his neck. "Well, your highness, it is all a bit strange. The Autumn Court is under the assumption that there is a dragon loose in the Under Realm."

"Impossible," denied Silje. "If that was the case, Queen Helena would have informed us. No, no, the fey court is simply trying to stir up trouble."

"That's what I thought, too," Henrik said quietly. "But, then, communication with the sorceress has been dodgy. The moment we tell her that Fritjof –"

The connection winked out. One moment Silje was before them, the next she was gone. Henrik started.

"Did she just hang up on you?" asked Christoffer. "I guess even queens can be rude."

"Try again," Aleks said, nodding to the horn in Henrik's hands.

Henrik brought it up for another short blast. The sound shot out and whistled through the air, but Silje didn't return. Henrik tried again and again. The night air before them remained stubbornly empty and dark.

Aleks looked at the others, foreboding thickening in his belly like a lump of overcooked oatmeal. "Nori is looking more and more right. A dragon named Fritjof really is on the loose."

Chapter Six: Trouble in Trolgar

"We can't warn anyone," Geirr said. "It's all on us to stop this dragon from breaking out. We're doomed."

"We've faced worse odds," said Christoffer, giving him a nudge.

"What are we going to do?" Zaria asked.

Aleks felt at a loss. It was a wholly strange experience for him. His hand went up to surreptitiously check his ear. Still pointy. He tried to pass off the movement as a scratch. He hoped nobody had noticed.

"What are we going to do?" Zaria asked, repeating herself.

Henrik squared his shoulders, preparing to say something to rouse them to the task ahead, when the woods around them erupted with war cries. From all sides came murderous looking mountain-trolls. They waved all manner of weapons over their heads, and several banged pots together. Before anyone could do a thing, they were captured. It was then that Jorkden, an enormous troll who also happened to be their leader, appeared in their midst.

"We meet again," he said with a wicked leer.

"The Wild Hunt," Geirr moaned, struggling against his captor. "We're going to be eaten."

Aleks stomped on the foot of the troll holding him and got walloped on the head for it. The jaw-jarring sensation just made him madder. He threw an elbow into the troll's solar plexus. The troll dropped him with a howl, but his freedom was short-lived for another grabbed him next.

"Let us go," he demanded angrily.

Jorkden shook his head and smiled wickedly, revealing a mouthful of teeth and protruding tusks. "You children and your escapes brought my trolden dishonor. We won't let you go. The Hunt never ends, although... it might be delayed."

"Delayed?" Filip repeated, taken aback. "We thought it was called off. It's been what – three years?"

Jorkden flashed a wolfish grin. "Not quite, but that doesn't matter." He turned away from them and barked at a female warrior covered in wolf skins to see to the bears.

"What does your king say about this?" Henrik spat, jerking one arm free. "Kafirr has gained new freedoms and provisions from the revised Dragomir Treaty for his efforts with Koll. Are you going to put that in jeopardy?"

"Kafirr is no longer king," Jorkden proclaimed, his expression wolfish. "I am king."

"No," Henrik said, unable to believe it. "That can't be true. He's twice your size."

Jorkden shrugged. "The bigger they are, the easier they are to hunt. One troll, no matter his size, can't defeat the horde."

"You fool," cried Zaria. "Let us go. There is a new dragon on the loose."

"I heard," Jorkden said, indicating the horn now held by a troll. "I don't care."

"You'll regret this," Aleks warned.

"Tie her up good. This one can do magic," he told her captors.

Zaria yelped as they followed his command. Filip struggled to reach her, but was hit for his efforts. When she was bound and gagged, Jorkden began commanding the others to take down and pack up their belongings. He swiped some of Zaria's meal and ate it whole, wiping juices from his chin.

Aleks saw Zaria squint and knew magic would be unleashed unless he stopped her now. Try as the trolls might, Zaria's thoughts, and therefore her magic, couldn't be tied up. He shook his head at her, the presence of magic raising the hairs on his skin as it danced along its surface.

She jerked back in confusion, the magic dying in her eyes. He nodded toward the bears, which were saddled again and grunting under the weight of their troll riders. If Zaria performed magic now, they wouldn't be able to escape.

He let out a sigh of relief when Zaria nodded, signaling she understood his message. The trolls tied the rest of them up similarly and marched them through the trees. The taste of the gag was horrible, like troll armpit sweat, but Aleks kept his complaints to himself, as his thoughts swirled wildly trying to come up with a plan for their escape.

His captor's hand shoved him hard in the back, and Aleks stumbled, nearly falling flat on his face. He shot the troll a glare, earning another shove. This was going to be a long night. He'd been looking forward to that feast and sleep under the stars.

At some point in the long march, Christoffer managed to sidle close to him. He pulled his gag down using his shoulder. "Why did you stop her?" he whispered. "She was going to bring the flash and bang right on top of their heads. We'd be back to finding Nori right now if she had."

Aleks removed his gag using the same method so he could answer. "Because then, they might knock her out and separate us from each other. I'm hoping to get us all out alive."

Christoffer frowned. "I didn't think about that."

"Back in line, humans," snarled a vicious looking troll with matted, blood-red hair. He whacked them both on the head and shoved them apart.

At least he didn't have to wear the gag anymore, Aleks thought, stretching his arms and hands, trying to get more blood flow to them. He was determined to keep alert and figure out Jorkden's endgame. He wondered too, if Kafirr was dead or alive, and whether the answer made any difference.

All through the night he and the others marched, until he was drooping and dragging his feet forward by sheer will. If the trolls would stop the march, even for a short while, it would be heaven. Ignoring his tired and aching feet, he looked to the others to see how they fared.

Zaria was practically sleep-walking. Christoffer kept stumbling over his feet. Filip and Geirr looked only slightly more clear-headed. Henrik, however, looked like he was playing at tiredness. His eyes were alert, and he watched the trolls and their friends in equal measure. Their eyes met, and Aleks saw an edge in Henrik's eyes he'd never seen before.

The Stag Lord must be aware, like him, that they'd been marched further than they needed to be and in a circle. Was it to tire them out or to confuse their sleepy minds about where they were? If the first, it was succeeding. If the second, it hadn't fooled everyone. Aleks prayed that whatever the case, they wouldn't be separated. They were going to need Zaria's magic to escape.

As dawn crept through the trees, the trolls finally guided them below the earth through a tree bolt hole. After Zaria and Christoffer had dropped from exhaustion, they'd been slung unceremoniously across the shoulders of a broad-chested troll with a smashed-in nose. Aleks hovered behind them, wishing his hands were in front of him so he could reach out to protect their heads from hitting a wall as the troll brushed by too close for comfort.

A little way ahead, between two burly trolls and with heads bent low, Henrik and Filip were conversing. Aleks could hear the soft murmurs of their voices. He looked around for Geirr and found him trudging along behind him, gag loose around his neck. He slowed so his friend could catch up.

"How are you doing?" he whispered.

Geirr grunted. "My feet hurt, my legs hurt, and my eyeballs could fall out from lack of sleep."

Aleks snickered. "Is that it? Did you catalogue everything?"

Geirr shook his head. "I could use a meal and a liter of water. I'd settle for a piece of fruit. I'm parched and hungry."

"They've been walking us in circles," Aleks said, looking over his shoulder.

Geirr half nodded. After a few long, slow, blinks he looked around. "Something isn't right," he said.

Aleks looked around, too. He frowned, trying to figure out what Geirr meant. He looked at his friend. Geirr canted his head in the trolls' direction.

"The last time the Wild Hunt captured us, they were all carousing and hooting and hollering. Are they tired, too, like us? Or is it something else?"

Aleks looked at Geirr. "You're not as dead on your feet as you look."

Geirr laughed weakly, it was more of a huff. "I'm highly observant. It's my super power."

Aleks snorted, but then grew serious. "Keep your wits about when we get to Trolgar. Take note of everything. We're going to need those keen observation skills."

Geirr tilted his head in acknowledgement, even as a troll pushed them apart. Ahead, Henrik and Filip were separated too, and Henrik's gag retied. Thinking of Geirr's words, Aleks watched the trolls, taking stock of each one. This time he didn't look at them to see where their escape might be; instead, he looked at them, really looked at them.

Each and every one of the trolls had tight expressions. They snorted and grunted, and, occasionally, pushed another one along who was flagging behind, but not one of them looked smug or proud or happy. Well no, there was one who did, and that one was Jorkden.

The massive troll marched in the middle of his trolden, his expression was full of gloating. His heavy fur cloak bristled about him like unassailable armor. His fists swung back and forth grandly, and his stride was purposeful and long. He looked like a warrior king returning home to the adulation of his people.

Light infiltrated the underground tunnel, and they were soon marched out into the humungous cavern that housed the great city-state of Trolgar. At the sight of them emerging from the tunnel, crowds along the streets broke out into cheers. The wall of noise was deafening, and Jorkden swelled in stature at the sound of their cries. He hailed them like a rock star greeting his fans.

Aleks could tell right away that it wasn't the vibrant crowd that had met them before with pride and cheer. This time the throng of trolls that greeted them looked like they had been ones beaten in warfare. They didn't look as good as Aleks and his friends. That was saying something, because he and the others were dead on their feet.

The crowd's cheers were strained and forced. Their eyes haunted. A wildness hung in the air, and the scent of desperation lingered almost like a physical odor. Every movement was jerky and frenetic, as if they were desperate not to become a target themselves. What could scare a mountain-troll?

As the group reached the center of the city, Aleks saw what was wrong. Hags and wolverines patrolled the crowds. Even though he knew they weren't related, the wolverines looked like shorter black and tan bears. Smaller than the trolls surrounding them, the wolverines and hags were nearly impossible to spot. Only the wolverines' gleaming red eyes revealed their presence, as they slinked between ankles and tails.

Aleks watched as the wolverines snapped at heels and the hags poked at backs, inciting greater noise from their victims. Not one troll, however, dared to step on the wolverines under their feet or swipe a tail at the hags. That wasn't normal. Why were the trolls putting up with such treatment?

Ahead, the palace loomed like a dark and foreboding presence. The palace itself was a mismatched structure composed from an amalgamation of different architecture and design styles. Parts were elegantly modeled while other parts were chunky and built like a fortress for defense. Deep crags that hadn't been there before pocked the palace's walls, as if something large and heavy had smashed into them.

The palace's tall gates stood sentinel like a silent presence. They were thrown wide open, guarded by a trio of banshees. As Aleks approached, they stared straight at him. This was the first time he had a chance to be so close to one, let alone three, and it gave him the heebie-jeebies.

Their faces were waxen and drawn, their eyes so sunken they appeared like empty sockets, and their pale white hair hung like tangled seaweed. Despite his best efforts to remain calm, his heartbeat quickened at the sight of them, and he found himself moving closer to the others to keep from walking too near them. They were worse than the hags.

The trolls tossed Aleks and his friends to the center of the courtyard. Henrik glared balefully at Jorkden, as the new troll king took his time mounting the palace steps to sit on the massive throne. Everything Jorkden did served to remind them who was in charge, and who no longer was.

"He's kind of puny isn't he?" whispered Christoffer. "You don't get that impression when he's standing."

Aleks nodded. The throne dwarfed Jorkden, but he knew pointing that out would only cause problems. As big as Jorkden was, he wasn't as mountainous as Kafirr. Trolls prized their rulers by their sheer size, which made Aleks wonder again how Jorkden had managed to overthrow his king.

"Why do you have hags and banshees patrolling?" Henrik asked, shrugging out of his gag. He strained against his captor's hold.

"They're evil," added Christoffer.

"Not evil, only misunderstood," Jorkden countered. "They've been given a place amongst the trolls. With us they can be free. They no longer have to hide in the dark corners of the earth."

"Just the darkest," muttered Geirr.

"What was that?" Jorkden demanded, leaning forward menacingly.

Geirr snapped his mouth shut and thrust his chin out. Jorkden nodded to one of his trolden. Geirr was slammed onto the ground. Zaria cried out behind her gag, fighting her guard. It was imperative she hid how her magic worked. Aleks had to distract her.

"What do you want?" he shouted, stepping over to Geirr, protecting him from another attack.

"What do I want? I want to hold a feast like we should have held when you were captured by the Wild Hunt the first time."

"He means to eat us," Geirr said, sitting up gingerly, testing his equilibrium along the way.

"Let the cook know the food has arrived," Jorkden called out to a female by the fountain holding a broom. "Take them to the dungeon. Leave their belongings here. I want that little metal egg."

Aleks fought the urge to run to his bag and take his stargazer. There was nothing he could do about it now. They would simply have to get it later.

"What about my firstborn?" barked a familiar voice from the rear. "The princess and her friends have been caught. Where's my girl?"

Jorkden sneered. "You didn't capture the princess and her little friends. I did. You haven't earned your daughter's freedom yet, traitor. Be glad I have given you such a chance and not thrown you down there in your own cell."

Aleks turned and saw Morvin trembling in rage. The troll's fists clenched and unclenched as he fought to keep his composure. He'd seen Morvin angry before on their first adventure in Trolgar. This time, though, Morvin's appearance was disturbing. His uniform was bloodstained and torn, his lower lip busted and bruised, and his mustache had seen better days. It looked like he'd been in the fight of his life and lost.

"How shall I prove myself to you?" Morvin bit out, his eyes and tone resentful.

"I'm sure you'll think of something," Jorkden said. "Now do as I said."

Morvin wrangled Henrik from the trolls guarding him and pushed him along, away from the courtyard and toward the dungeons. He and the others were roughly prodded into following. Aleks looked forward to being in the cells, because that's when his plan for escape could happen.

"Don't get any funny ideas, either," Jorkden called out, startling Aleks who for a moment thought the troll had heard his thoughts, until he added, "Keep the princess separate from her friends. I don't want her loose to use her magic."

Aleks let out a sigh of relief. They still didn't suspect Zaria's true talent with magic. As long as they didn't knock her unconscious, they would be able to escape. He hoped that the trolls would be overconfident, so she'd be placed in a cell near them.

Trolls appeared in the hallway wearing badly fitting king's uniforms. There was something vaguely familiar about them. Aleks stared at their faces until the memories clicked. These trolls were from the original Wild Hunt.

There was Thorkel, a troll with a big nose; and Mangus, a bully of a troll with thick, dark, eyebrows; and Groul, a short, stout, troll with fists like hams and an unkempt beard. He, Filip, and Geirr had once fought Mangus and Groul, only to lose spectacularly. The only one missing from that fight was Yorgish.

"Looky here," Mangus sneered, a grin twisting his lips. "It's the once mighty Morvin, of the esteemed

Black-Tailed Ribcage Butchers House. How the mighty have fallen. What are you now?"

"He's a rotten Yellow-Belly Boot Licker," Thorkel said, guffawing at his own joke. "You're not so tough now are you, Boot Licker?"

Morvin's nostrils flared and his jaw flexed, but when he spoke his voice was civil, like a reined-in man-eating tiger. "Move aside. Jorkden has requested these children be shown to the dungeons."

"King Jorkden," Mangus corrected, cracking his knuckles.

"He's not king yet," Morvin replied blandly. "He still has to beat King Kafirr in a one-on-one fight to claim the crown."

Mangus made a move to punch Morvin, but decided at the last moment to pull back. Aleks thought that was smart, because even beaten up, Morvin was a force to reckon with. Plus, he had at least three stones on the other troll.

"Watch your back, traitor," Mangus warned, pulling Thorkel and Groul along behind him.

Groul licked his lips, his teeth yellow like sulfur. "Bye-bye tasty morsels. I'll be eating you later, scooping you up with a nice hearty bread."

He snapped at Henrik, who barely flinched, but his minute reaction still made Groul laugh. Henrik turned his steely-eyed gaze on Morvin. The troll beckoned to the other guards, and the six friends were dragged through to the dungeons.

Chapter Seven: The Crownless King

Down in the dungeons Aleks got his second wind, perking up as Morvin slammed the door shut on Zaria's prison cell. It was hard not to be jolted awake after the bang it made. Morvin growled for the guards to go ahead, while he secured the boys in a cell across from her. Aleks was grateful they wouldn't have to find each other in the dungeons later.

The trolls scurried out, eager to get away from the roaming banshees that walked the dungeon's corridors with their eerie moaning. One of the banshees stopped beside Morvin and cried out. Aleks cringed, trying to cover his ears with his shoulders, wishing again for use of his hands.

Her cry was ear-splittingly loud and raked against his spine like feedback through a microphone. Morvin snarled at her, adding another layer to the unholy din. She hissed reproachfully, and then drifted off. When she was gone, the troll wiggled a finger in his ear and shuddered.

"I hate those things," he said to them. "Jorkden uses banshees to patrol the dungeons. Mind your manners around them, or they'll burst your eardrums with their screeching."

Henrik looked straight at him. "What's going on?"

Morvin's eyes flickered after the retreating banshee. Under his breath, he said, "Jorkden's lost his mind. He augmented his Wild Hunt with the banshees and hags. Then before anyone knew or could guess, he came sweeping through the city with his new Wild Hunt and took it by force. We were wholly unprepared and in the end it didn't matter how hard we fought. We were overpowered."

"Where's Kafirr?" Henrik asked. "What happened to him? You said they still had to fight before Jorkden could claim the throne."

"Jorkden used the Wild Hunt to take the throne. Kafirr used the mountain to send them flying, but there were too many. He could not keep up with their numbers. In time they wrestled him to the ground and threw him in the dungeons. That way," he said, tilting his head to the right. "He's in the deepest, darkest, spot, guarded night and day."

"Why doesn't he use the mountain now to break out?" asked Christoffer.

"The cell is lined top to bottom with iron," Morvin explained. "He's completely cut off from the mountain. He has no power down there."

"Why didn't you rescue him? Have you been on Jorkden's side all along?" Geirr accused.

Morvin opened their cell and roughly shoved them inside. "Bite your tongue. Don't you think the great houses tried? Our attempt failed, and Jorkden retaliated. He took our firstborns and locked them up down here, somewhere where we haven't been able to find them. My Kanutte is down here at the mercy of those creatures."

"Your daughter," Aleks said. "I could find her. I could find all of them. Let us go. We can help."

Morvin hesitated, but a distant wail reminded him what was at stake. He maneuvered the boys to the walls where extra security hung in the form of shackles. He pressed them into chains and took off their old rope bindings. Rattling them, Aleks stretched his arms in front of him with a groan.

"I dare not risk it," he said. He looked almost sad. "Your failure would be the Black-Tails undoing. Already, Jorkden hangs onto his power by threatening our children. No, no. We must wait for the Battle of Kings. Kafirr will win it, and all will be right again. The others might not agree, but waiting is our best option, no matter how tempting your offer is. It's too big a risk to take. We simply have to wait."

"Jorkden's cheating," Henrik said quietly. "He should have fought Kafirr one-on-one the first day."

Morvin's eyes narrowed to slits. "Don't you think I know that? We all know that, but he has our children. He has them at the mercy of those –" He jabbed a finger behind him toward the bars, "– those *things*."

"Why didn't you get help?" Henrik asked. "The dwarf king owes Kafirr a debt from the Battle of Koll's Bane. Flein should have been told."

"Is that what they're calling it?" asked Christoffer. "That's freaking brilliant!"

"Not now," Henrik said to him, and Christoffer made a motion to zip his lips and throw away the key.

"The Long-Eared Bone Crunchers and Great-Footed Bear Bashers tried to get out a message through the dwarf mirror a week ago, but they were caught and the mirror smashed. Not just that mirror, but all of them. When you were brought through the city, didn't you notice how dark it was down here?"

"Now that you mention it…" Filip said. "It did seem fairly dark. A lot more torchlight. Is it because it was barely daybreak?"

"No," Morvin said, tightening the last of their chains, and walked out of the cell. He gazed at them with sorrow. "He's stolen our light; he's taken our future. All of the great houses' firstborns are down here. My hands are tied. We won't enjoy eating you at the feast, but we will eat you all the same."

"You're making a terrible mistake," Henrik shouted, rattling his chains. "You can't give up. You have to fight. All of you must, or you will perish."

There was no response from Morvin. He had left them to their fate. A low, keening wail filled the night, as the banshees moved about in the dark. They were all alone. Henrik slumped against the wall, his antlered-hood pulling low over his brow.

"Can I use magic now?" asked Zaria softly from the other cell.

"Do it. Be fast," Aleks said, knowing that there was little time to spare.

He heard a chink and a clink, as metal fell away. Then a low groan reverberated as her cell door opened. Aleks hoped that the banshees would think it was one of their own calling out. Another click and their prison door opened.

"As tired as I am, I'll be glad to get moving," Christoffer said with a yawn. "Let me loose."

"I'll get to you in a second," Zaria said, yawning, too. She flapped her hand at him. "Stop that. You'll get us all started, and we'll fall asleep down here and get stuck as *soup du jour.*"

Filip grinned blearily at her, as she undid him first. He was closest to the door. She released Christoffer and Geirr next. Their shackles unlocked and fell with sharp clanks against the walls.

"Thank you, Princess," Henrik said as she went over and removed his restraints.

She caught the shackles before they banged against the stone surface. Henrik stretched and then began checking his pockets. He pulled out the stargazer and waved it at them.

"How did you get that?" Aleks asked, as Zaria released him next. He was too happy to care about the theft. He rubbed his wrists and ankles.

"One of the trolls already had the horn, and Jorkden wanted the stargazer. I knew we couldn't let him have it, so I *stumbled* into the troll carrying your bag and palmed it early on just in case we lost our things. I didn't think to do the same with the mirror, though."

The 'stumbled' was said with air quotes.

"That's all right," Filip said. "The mirror and horn were getting spotty reception half the time anyway. The stargazer is what counts. I was worried our parents would become aware of our adventure."

"Maybe we should leave it hidden safely away somewhere next time," Geirr said. "Then we won't have to worry about thieving trolls."

"It was useful, though, against the fairies," Christoffer reminded. "Better to keep it on us."

"I have the Drakeland Sword," Zaria said, pulling a shrunken sword and scabbard from her pocket. "I shrunk this after riding on the bears for a while, and I'm glad I did, because it's still in our possession."

"My knees thank you for shrinking it," Christoffer said. At Aleks' look, he explained, "The sword's scabbard kept banging into me as the bear moved."

The Drakeland Sword was designed to tackle dragons. It fearlessly approached battle with them, something Aleks had witnessed firsthand. It was made from a special ore that was also used to power dwarfish mirrors. Wielding it in her hand and using her magic, Zaria had taken on Koll and won. It would be essential in the fight against Fritjof.

"We need to get out of here," Geirr prompted, as a skin-crawling howl sluiced through the air.

Filip nodded at Zaria, as she tied the now enlarged scabbard and sword around her waist. "We could also use some weapons. Can you help us out, Zar-Zar?"

"We need to rescue those troll kids," Zaria said, whipping up several weapons and passing them out. Aleks took a familiar bow and quiver of arrows. "Saving those firstborns might be our only chance to stop Jorkden's rotten reign in Trolgar."

Henrik nodded, securing his new sword. "We can't leave them trapped. The great houses are unable to act while their children are held captive by him. Unless they all act, the mountain-trolls are doomed."

"Lead the way, mate," Filip invited, indicating the open prison door with his new, short sword.

Aleks pointed to the stargazer and Henrik dropped it into his outstretched hand. He pocketed it and left the cell. Out in the corridor he went right, following the path that Morvin had said led to Kafirr. At the first junction his mind began busily creating a mental map.

He filled in several pieces of it from their first trip through these dank dungeons.

He followed the paths in his head and guided the others to where he thought the troll children would be kept. Once or twice they had to duck into an open cell to avoid roaming banshees. Their haunted faces and hidden eyes affected the mood of the group. The joy of escape died at their pitiful wailing, which rang like hammers in their ears and crawled along their spines like nails on chalkboard. Aleks suppressed another shudder, as a wail bounced along the corridors.

"I wish I had earplugs," Geirr muttered darkly, covering his ears as they watched a listless banshee glide-float away from them.

"Good idea," Zaria said. She held out her hands and several pairs of earplugs appeared.

There was a rush to grab them. Aleks took his gratefully and popped them into place. A low aching thrum he hadn't been aware of vanished immediately. He sighed in relief.

Aleks led them away from the banshee, and they slipped like shadows to the floor below, taking a twisting, turning staircase to a lower dungeon. As they approached the end of a wing, Aleks slowed, sensing this was his destination.

He kept an eye out for the guards that were sure to be on duty. With the earplugs, however, he couldn't make out their cries. As his eyes adjusted to the dimness, he saw shadows flicker along the floor.

"I got this," Henrik said, touching Aleks' shoulder and sliding around him and up to where the shadows melted in and out of view.

He disappeared around the corner. They heard and saw nothing for a few tense moments. Then his antlered head popped around the corner. He waved them over and Zaria ran to join him first. Reaching the Stag Lord, her hand flew to her mouth covering a horrified gasp.

Aleks looked and saw three banshees knocked out on the ground, lying in awkward positions. His mouth dropped in surprise. Their pale locks were shorn to the quick. Hair laid scattered like rushes all over the floor. Henrik stood there, chest heaving, sword at his side. He took out his earplugs, palming them, and motioned for everyone else to do the same.

"What happened?" asked Christoffer, gazing agape at the creatures on the ground. "What's with the hair?"

"Without their hair, they lose their voice. They won't be able to scream at us."

"Who's out there?" an angry voice rumbled with the threat of malevolence.

"Kafirr, is that you?" Henrik asked, moving closer to the solid iron door.

"Is that the new Stag Lord?" the voice returned, its tone changing to one of wonder.

"Aye," said Henrik, pulling open the small window at the top of the cell door and peering inside.

"I thought you were taking us to the troll kids," Geirr said, looking bewildered and trying to peer past Henrik into the cell.

Aleks didn't respond. He was confused. He'd meant to take them to the troll kids. How had he taken them here instead? He ran through the mental map trying to figure out the source of his error, but he couldn't. Was this the start of him losing his fey-gifts? Or was this Fritjof messing with him? Or something else? He shook his head. He had no idea.

"King Kafirr," Zaria said, moving closer and grabbing the door handle. "I can get you out of there."

"No, don't," he said hoarsely, his voice weak. They heard a shuffling sound and suddenly a great eye peeked out at them from the window. "Save the firstborn children."

"We can save you all," she said. "Where are they?"

"There are too many of them to save us all. The children come first. Leave the banshees here as a distraction. The rest will come running to check on me to ensure I'm still trapped here."

"You have to be rescued," Filip said. "Without your strength, how can you fight Jorkden?"

Kafirr laughed wheezily. "No mountain-troll will accept a king who didn't win his crown in a one-on-one combat. The power of the individual is what we respect in Trolgar."

"But we heard he wasn't feeding you," Zaria said, objecting. "How long have you been down here? How long has this been going on?"

"I've been imprisoned almost a year," he replied. "At least I think it's been a year. What month is it?"

"September," said Aleks.

Kafirr closed his eyes. "More than a year, then. I've been stuck down here since August."

"So long?" she said, dismayed.

"Don't worry, Princess," said Kafirr. "Even weak as I am from starvation, Jorkden can't beat me on his own and that'll be his downfall. They'll see him as the weakling he is."

"How can you manage?" she asked.

Aleks wanted to know that, too. Thirteen months was an awfully long time to go without food.

"I'm an Iron-Bellied Stone Eater, and us Stone Eaters never cave into hunger. We'd eat the very earth if we must to survive," Kafirr said backing away from the door to grab something. There was a great cracking sound. He returned and held out a lump of metal through the bars. "My mother weaned me on iron ore, that's why my teeth are strong and black. I've been eating what iron I can break off from my cell. It keeps me strong. If I eat enough of it, I might be able to reach the mountain behind the cell and break out."

"You've been trying to do that for a year. Why wait? Jorkden's merciless, when it comes to protecting his power," Henrik said, trying to persuade the troll king. "Come with us. Let us get you to safety amongst your faithful houses. They need you."

Kafirr shook his head. "I won't go with you, not without the children, and if I come, we'll be spotted. I'm too large to hide. They won't be safe. Leave me."

"You don't know what he's like," Aleks said. "You don't know what's he's doing to your people."

The troll king's eyes narrowed. "Don't I? He rules with an iron fist, because he knows the great houses would overthrow him if he showed one second of weakness. I know it, too, which is why even the slightest infractions are deemed traitorous. Jorkden would rather kill us all than lose to me. Save their firstborns, and the resistance can start again in earnest. Give my trolden back their hope."

"We can't leave you here," Geirr protested. "Who knows when your trolden could rescue you?"

"Leave me," Kafirr said. "Do it now. The children are back the way you came and in the offshoot halfway back toward the stairs. Sometimes they are moved, but it's been a while since I've heard them in the hallways. This might be our – *your* – only chance to rescue them all."

"This is unacceptable," Zaria said, wrinkling her nose. "Stand back. If you won't let me rescue you, at the very least I'm going feed you."

Kafirr vanished from sight in a blink. Thudding and thumping noises began almost at once as Zaria concentrated on the cell. Then a sucking, slurping sound took over.

Aleks got closer and peered inside the small window. Inside the cramped cell a mound of meats fell from the ceiling and piled high on the floor. The troll king attacked the food like a starving beast. Whole ham hocks and ribs were swallowed down, bones and all. As fast as he was wolfing down the food, Zaria was faster. The cell filled nearly to bursting.

"Thank you, Princess," Kafirr said, his words muffled by a rack of lamb. "It is a feast fit for a king." He belched. "Now go. There's no time to lose."

"We'll see to it," Henrik said, sweeping the others away using his cloak.

Aleks glanced one last time at the crownless king. Kafirr stared at him with cold, clear, ice-blue eyes. His black hair and beard, long and tangled around his face, masked his expression. He watched Aleks with a queer look in his eyes.

"Stay strong," Aleks murmured, earning a snort of disgust in response.

"Stay sharp, Changeling," he replied. "I cannot help you from here. Don't get lost."

"What do you mean?" Aleks asked.

"Your sixteenth birthday is not far away," Kafirr said knowingly. "You don't have much longer to decide who you are."

Aleks wanted to protest that he had decided, but angry cries pierced the gloom. He looked around, trying to pinpoint their source. He thought they came from the direction his friends had gone. Kafirr snarled low in his throat, his hands clenching into tight fists. The howls obviously affected him, and

Aleks knew then it was the troll kids howling for help in the distance.

"Go," the troll king hissed. "Save them. Go, and don't come back."

Chapter Eight: The Firstborn

Aleks turned at once and ran, racing to catch up with his friends all the while stuffing his earplugs back in place. He dodged around corners, distracted so much by the impact of Kafirr's rough words that he nearly crashed headlong into Filip's back.

His lovelorn friend raised an eyebrow. "You all right there, mate?"

Aleks slowed down and caught his breath. "I'm fine, but those howls weren't the banshees. They were from those troll kids. We have to hurry."

"Are you certain?" asked Zaria.

Aleks nodded grimly. "Kafirr was furious. He said not to come back for him."

"Then that's what we'll do," Henrik said, stepping aside for Aleks to pass.

At the front, Aleks took a steadying breath, and let his innate magic paint him a picture of the dungeons. They had to find an offshoot halfway between Kafirr and the stairwell that had brought them to this lower level. He could almost see it and took off for it, keeping his fears to himself that he might be losing the gift that made him useful. He also pushed aside the part of him that worried about this worry. Normalcy was what he wanted after all, wasn't it?

Henrik ran apace with him, sword drawn at the ready. They took one hallway and then another. Suddenly, Aleks could see in his mind the correct path to the kids. It lit up in his mind like a beacon. He grabbed Henrik's arm and stopped him.

"We've gone too far," he said at the Stag Lord's questioning look.

Henrik turned around without comment and Aleks told the others when to stop running. A small alcove at the start of the hall hid a big secret. Behind the torch-bearing sconce lay a nearly hidden passage.

The fit was extremely tight, and Zaria had to shrink Henrik's cloak so its golden antlers would fit through the space. Christoffer grabbed the torch as he passed by, and it was a good thing he did, for the other side was dark as pitch.

Aleks' eyes adjusted to the torchlight once in the corridor. His insides crawled at the sight before him. Beside him Zaria gasped in horror. Two troll girls were held in the clutches of a group of banshees. One troll girl was white as a ghost, and the other partially petrified, her skin turning into stone. Both girls' eyes were glazed over, their fight gone.

He was glad to be wearing the earplugs, which muted the banshees' torturous wails. The little sound that leaked through caused his skin to erupt into gooseflesh. He rubbed his arms. A dulled clamor drew his attention to the cells that formed the end of the hall. Hands reached out, desperate to stop what was happening. That shook him into action.

He plucked an arrow from his wrist-quiver and raised his bow, firing into the banshees, appreciative now more than ever for the hours of lessons and practice he had put in over the years. The arrow stuck one in the shoulder. She arched her back and cried out.

The two nearest her spun around at once and shrieked. Their gaping mouths split and widened. From the corner of his eye, Aleks saw Filip flinch. It truly was a gruesome sight. Kind of cool, but incredibly creepy. Their sunken black eyes didn't help matters either.

"Cut the hair," Henrik shouted, although, through the earplugs, the sound reached Aleks' ears as if he had shouted underwater.

The Stag Lord rushed forward, sword raised to strike, with Zaria hot on his heels, the Drakeland Sword in her grip. They charged at the banshees, blocking Aleks' clean shot. He tensed, feeling his muscles lock into place and knew he had to drop his position or risk fatigue. He eased the bowstring, and let out a long, slow, steadying breath.

Filip got one of the banshees by the hair, his short sword poised to strike. She screamed and clawed at him, raking long nails down his arms, leaving welts, but it was too late. He'd cut her hair length by half, and she fell to the ground, crying. Christoffer and Geirr teamed up against another, and she went down on a silent scream.

As his friends thinned the banshees, the troll girls began to revive. The troll who'd been white as a ghost, now had color flooding her cheeks and an angry twist to her mouth. The one who'd been partially petrified was slowly returning to flesh and blood. The pale troll dragged the other to a safe distance. Aleks watched them; both were pained by every shriek splitting the air, impeding their recovery.

An opening shot appeared, and Aleks repositioned. Sighting down the shaft, he let go and watched the arrow fly. His target moved, and the arrow skimmed by her cheek, leaving a black gash. The banshee turned and rushed him. Aleks rushed to notch another arrow. She leapt at him and Aleks flinched, his arrow shot wildly, missing its mark.

He braced for the blow, but the banshee's attack was cut short. Geirr tackled her from behind, his momentum bringing them to the earthen floor. The two landed as if they had belly-flopped into a pool. Winded, the banshee had no breath left to scream. Geirr scrambled, using his knife to slice through her pale white hair. She slumped, defeated.

"Thanks," Aleks said gratefully, reaching out a hand.

"No problem," Geirr said, accepting his hand up.

They turned to watch the last of the fight. Two banshees remained. Henrik and Filip went after one, while Zaria and Christoffer got the other. When the last one fell, the silence was a shock, even through the earplugs. Bodies littered the floor. Tangled white hair clung to every surface, sticking to clothes, shoes, skin, walls, and floor. Christoffer even spat out a mouthful of it.

"Who are you?" the pallid troll girl demanded.

Aleks took out his earplugs to hear her better. He pointed to himself, and said, "I'm Aleks, and we're here to rescue you at King Kafirr's behest. These are my friends."

"You're the Stag Lord," the no-longer petrified girl accused, pointing at Henrik.

"Guilty," Henrik said, confused. "Who are you?"

"I'm Gisken," said the troll who'd spoken first. As her color returned, red marks appeared on her face and neck. "I'm firstborn to the honorable Red-Throated Blood Drinkers House. This is Kanutte."

"Gisken," Kanutte hissed, swiping a long black tail at the other troll. "We're down here, because of these wretched weaklings."

"You're free because of us, you mean," Geirr said, crossing his arms.

"And you're not turned to stone, anymore," Christoffer added, tucking away his daggers. "We should at least get a thanks for risking our lives."

"Never," hissed Kanutte. "I'd sooner claw your eyes out than thank you."

"Morvin, your father, is worried about you," Henrik said in his most reasonable voice. "We need to free your compatriots and get to your father. He'll know what to do next."

"We don't need your help," Kanutte insisted, dragging Gisken backwards. "Go away."

"Knottie," Christoffer said, "Can I call you Knottie? Or maybe, Canny? Taughtie?"

"Can it, if you want to live to breathe another second," she snarled, swiping her tail menacingly.

"I thought you said your name was Can Not, not Can It," Christoffer said with a merry twinkle in his eyes.

He clearly ignored the memo to not aggravate a troll.

Kanutte raised her fist to punch him. "Make fun of my name one more time, pipsqueak."

"Look, be reasonable," Aleks said, cutting off whatever Christoffer would have said next. He didn't need his friend antagonizing Kanutte further. They needed her cooperation. "How long have you been down here?"

Kanutte sneered at him, but her friend stopped her from speaking. Gisken looked at the trolls locked in the cells behind her. She said, "Close to ten months for some of us."

"Don't be offended," Christoffer said, putting Aleks instantly on his guard. "You're so much bigger than us, and we had to squeeze through the entrance to get in here. How did you guys make it?"

"They walled up the entrance after the older ones had been placed down here," Gisken said, her eyes faraway, haunted.

"Only the banshees could reach us," Kanutte added bitterly. "My father tried rescuing Zorka and Regnor, but was caught. That's how I ended up here."

"I'm about to get you all out," Zaria said.

"You don't even have a key," Kanutte huffed. "How are we all supposed to get out?"

"Couldn't you break down the doors?" Filip asked. "I mean, we got out from down here once ourselves."

"By digging a hole," Gisken said evenly while shoving Kanutte off her. "That was clever of you to find a way out. It helps to be small I suppose."

Kanutte rolled her eyes. "The dungeon was retrofitted after that disaster to stop any escape by the same method."

"Stop gabbing like girls and get us out of here," a tough-sounding troll said from within a cell.

"Shut up, Regnor. This is why nobody wants to go out with you," Gisken said, winking coyly at Henrik.

"Plus, you stink," Kanutte added. "It's not just dungeon funk either."

148

Henrik coughed lightly into his hand, and stowed his sword. "Let's get everyone out, shall we?"

"You still haven't said how," Kanutte grumped, folding her beefy arms. "It's not like we can pull the doors from their moorings."

"We tried that," Gisken explained. "Many, many, times. Just look at my hands. My nails are ruined."

"Your mother would be horrified to hear that," Regnor said. "Trolls don't care about their nails."

A new voice spoke out, accompanied by a big, beefy hand which wrapped around the cell's small opening. "I don't care how you get us out, just get us out."

"What Falkor said," Gisken said, moving aside.

"That's your cue, Princess," Henrik said, motioning Zaria forward.

"This won't take but a moment," Zaria said, walking toward the trolls.

"Princess?" Kanutte said, raising an eyebrow in derision. "More like street urchin. You lack the proper posture, clothes, and speech. You're not fit to use the Drakeland Sword. Who's your mother? She should have taught you better."

"That's Princess Zaria of the Under Realm," Aleks said dryly. "Who are you to act like she's nobody?"

"Aleks, it's okay," Zaria said, waving him off. "She probably just didn't know."

"She knew," Gisken said, shooting daggers with her eyes at Kanutte. "She's simply ignoring her breeding to be rude, as usual."

Zaria, taken aback for a moment, blinked before shrugging it off. "We don't have much time. Let me through, so I can undo the doors."

Gisken pulled a reluctant Kanutte aside, and Zaria slipped by. Aleks watched her advance, keeping a wary eye on Morvin's daughter. Kanutte did not like them, that much was obvious, but he didn't understand why. She would have to be watched. The dark-tailed troll could easily break Zaria's arm without even trying, if she had a mind to do so.

"You two should watch the main corridor," Aleks said, nodding to Geirr and Filip. "See if anybody is coming. Our fight wasn't exactly quiet, as you know."

They nodded. Geirr stuffed his earplugs back in as he headed for the entrance. Aleks ignored their progress over the listless bodies to watch Zaria do her bit. He hoped she'd use her hands and hide the true nature of her magic. It was important she still kept up the pretense that she had her mother's magical gifts.

When she looked over her shoulder at them, he made a twirling hand motion. She caught his eye and nodded. He grinned, glad that she was easy to communicate with. Zaria raised her hands and waved them about in an elaborate gesture. It was so fake he nearly laughed aloud and ruined her performance.

She had two of the four cells unlocked in a trice. A big, burly, teenage troll with heavy eyebrows, slightly bowed legs, and a charmingly broken nose, came out first. He clapped her heartily on the back, which sent her flying from the sheer force.

"Oops, my bad," he said, picking her up. "Name's Falkor."

"Don't help her," Kanutte snipped, her eyes flashing with jealousy.

"Love you, too, Knottie," he said affably, dusting off Zaria, and ignoring the bristling female troll a few feet away.

"So I was right about your nickname," Christoffer said, earning a hiss from the girl.

Falkor ambled toward them, scooching Zaria along in the crook of his arm. He stopped to shake Aleks' and Henrik's hands. "I, for one, am glad to get out of that stink-hole."

Aleks laughed, because Falkor did smell foul, as if he had indeed emerged from a nasty stink-hole. He smelled exactly like rancid meat. It clung to him like a second skin. Zaria's face was skewed up into a twitching placid expression, as if she was trying not to make a face or have her eyes water.

Luckily for Aleks, his mother always made him chop up the onions for dinner, so he was used to his eyes watering. He breathed past the stench and kept his composure. Christoffer, though, had to take a discreet step back and breathe through a sleeve.

"Someone's coming," Geirr warned, peeking out. "Everyone be quiet."

All in the hallway fell silent in an instant. Trolls, humans, Stag Lord, changeling, and sorceress – all stilled. Nobody dared to move. Aleks strained his ears to hear and had to quickly insert his earplugs. A swarm of banshees lamented, howling and wailing so loudly that Aleks could hear the screech, like a high pitched whine, through his earplugs.

"We better not wait for them to get here," Henrik said, unsheathing his sword.

Falkor nodded and started herding younger troll kids from his cell. They couldn't be more than the human equivalent of eight years old. Their tusks were too big for their mouths, their eyes wide and innocent, with straight noses unbroken from tussles or fist-a-cuffs.

Zaria unlocked the last of the cells, and three other trolls about the same age as Falkor, Kanutte, and

Gisken appeared, herding more kids. A girl with long ears, tie-dyed hair, and an eyebrow piercing shepherded two young boys. Gisken hailed her as Zorka. A troll, lanky and hairy as a wolf, guided one young troll out of his cell. He was Modolf. Regnor was the third, with a needle-sharp tail and shortly cropped hair. He stepped out on his own.

All in all, there were twelve trolls plus the six of them, making for a very crowded and cramped hallway. Aleks pushed his way to the front, joining Filip and Geirr by the entrance. He peered out, checking one way and then the other.

He felt instinctively that this was the best time to try an escape, and dragged his friends with him. He heard Henrik tell Zaria to knock down the bricks. Kanutte made a rude noise about magic being for weaklings, and a second later, a large boom and cloud of dust filled the hallway.

"Was that really necessary?" Zaria asked, clearly annoyed. "Look at the mess you've made!"

"Not to mention the noise," muttered Christoffer.

Aleks looked back and saw the two girls glaring at each other, covered head-to-toe in dust and debris. Falkor separated them, shoving Kanutte through the opening. She balked and braced herself against either side of the gaping hole.

"It's not big enough yet," she protested.

"Should have let the sorceress do her magic then," Falkor said, unsympathetic. "Turn sideways."

One by one the trolls escaped by squeezing sideways through the opening. Aleks watched for a moment, but a tug on his elbow reminded him to get moving. He raced to the stairs, Geirr and Filip right behind him, and they ran up them, two at a time.

A loud roar of rage blasted through the dungeons. That had to be Kafirr causing a distraction, having heard Kanutte take down the wall. The keening cries from the banshees shifted, and Aleks knew they were heading for the troll king, giving them the extra time they needed to escape.

When the others caught up, he asked, "Where to from here?"

Kanutte said, "My father's house."

"Too dangerous," Falkor replied, rejecting the suggestion. "Jorkden is watching him like a hawk."

"I want to see my father," she insisted, stamping a foot on top of his.

Falkor grunted, his dark eyebrows pulling lower into a furious frown as he hopped on one foot. "Knottie, you know it's not safe. We need to get to the resistance. We'll be of more help to our families if we're there."

Christoffer shook his head. "How come this one can call you Knottie, but I can't?"

"They're dating," Zorka said, laughing and tossing her rainbow-colored hair. "Kanutte would tear anyone else apart for even thinking of her as Knottie. Isn't that right?"

Kanutte refused to respond, but her furious glare was answer enough, causing the other trolls to laugh. Falkor put an arm around her shoulders and cajoled her out of her stiffness. She melted a little in his arms, much to Aleks' surprise. He hadn't expected that.

"Falkor's right," Modolf said, bringing the topic back to the point. His voice was sonorous like a wolf's growl, deep and low with a slight lilt. "We need to get to the market."

"Fine," Kanutte huffed, "but we don't need tagalongs." Her glare indicated Zaria and the others.

Aleks shook his head. "We should stick together, at least until the market. Kafirr wanted us to see you all to safety."

"You would have been better off rescuing him," Modolf said. "If he could get into a fight with Jorkden, he would win, and all this would be over."

"He wouldn't let us," Zaria explained. "He said you were the hope of Trolgar, and you had to come first."

A fierce, angry, growl skittered up the stairs, causing them all to look back. Regnor opened his mouth to speak, when a shout rang down upon their heads.

"I knew it," Mangus leered, stopping in his tracks. Yorgish and Groul appeared on either side of him. He cracked his knuckles. "I knew Morvin was the worst sort of traitor. He let you go, didn't he, Princess? You're dead meat, and so is he when we tell King Jorkden. Get them!"

"RUN!" Aleks shouted, spurring everyone into action.

He pushed Zaria and Filip forward, as the older troll kids grabbed the youngsters and ran. The smallest kids were tossed over broad shoulders as if they weighed no more than sacks of potatoes.

Aleks swung around with his bow at the ready and fired into the advancing trolls. They dodged his arrows and ignored the ones that had landed their marks, merely grunting at the pain. Troll skin was notoriously tough to penetrate. He kept firing anyway, trying to give the others enough of a lead.

The three trolls closed the gap, and Aleks ceased firing arrows, not willing to risk getting captured again. He turned and sprinted after the others, catching up with Henrik and Christoffer, both of whom had lingered in case he needed help.

"Your aim sucks," Christoffer said, by way of greeting.

Winded, Aleks said, "We can trade. You want the bow?"

"Heck no," he said, clutching his daggers and grinning. "My aim is worse. At least you've practiced to be as bad as you are."

"Let's go," Henrik said, directing them through the remaining hallways up to the ground floor of the palace. Aleks didn't even mind, thankful for once not to be leading.

"Are the others safe?" asked Aleks.

"The others are out," Henrik confirmed.

"Good," Aleks panted. "Now it's our turn."

Chapter Nine: A Leap of Faith

The three of them had no time for stealth. Aleks was on his third or fourth wind, when Mangus bellowed and called down the troops the minute he emerged after them from the dungeons, ruining their attempt to sneak away unseen. Aleks, Christoffer, and Henrik had been crouch-running by the fountain, when a fresh wave of palace guards, banshees, and hags appeared from their posts. True to form, they were spotted immediately.

The pursuit was on, and the chances for escape weren't in their favor. Henrik and Christoffer broke from their positions and sprinted toward the fast-closing palace doors. Aleks took a few shots with his arrows and sprinted after them. Henrik swung his sword at a few hags and their wolverines.

With a vicious snarl, as scary as any bear's, one of the creatures jumped on Christoffer, sending him sprawling. They rolled and tumbled for control, the wolverine spitting and snarling. Christoffer's eyes nearly bugged out of his face, as he struggled to keep the wolverine's snapping jaws from his neck.

"Get this thing off me!" Christoffer grunted.

Aleks shouted to Henrik and fired arrows as fast as he could to protect his friends, as the Stag Lord went to help. He speared the wolverine through the back with an arrow. It reared, making a noise that turned Aleks' insides to ice. Henrik pushed past a hag and pulled the thing off Christoffer, tossing it aside. Then he reached down and dragged him onto his feet.

"Is anyone scared spitless? No? Just me?" Christoffer wheezed, hands on his throat, as if double-checking it was still intact.

"You're not going anywhere," Mangus said, blocking their path to the palace doors, which clanged shut like a death knell.

Aleks shot at him, but Mangus batted it away with a heavy fist. If only troll skin wasn't practically impenetrable. What good were arrows when even some bullets barely made an impact? He had few arrows left and couldn't risk any of them not landing their mark. He had to be strategic. He wouldn't waste another on Mangus or his trolden.

"We need another way out," Henrik said, even as they all backed away from the trolls as a single unit.

A circle of wolverines pressed in on them. Christoffer eyed them worriedly. Aleks tried to concentrate to find a solution to their situation, but all he saw were rows and rows of gleaming serrated teeth and pairs and pairs of glaring crimson eyes. Everywhere he looked, there was danger. Escape seemed impossible.

"Any time now would be good," Christoffer said, a little frantic, as a wolverine snapped at his ankles. He jumped out of the way.

Aleks looked around desperately, swinging his head from side to side. He spotted an empty staircase to the ramparts. "There," he shouted, pointing.

They took off as one. Christoffer and Henrik slashed at the wolverines. Aleks dodged another and hopped over the fountain. He slipped by a trio of hags, feeling the air move as they snapped shut their outstretched claws inches from him. Careening into the stairs, he quickly righted and dashed up them two at a time with Christoffer and Henrik at his back.

The wolverines clambered after them, their feet scrabbling on the smooth stone. Aleks reached the top of the rampart and looked out over the city. Straight ahead was the city's wide thoroughfare. It offered zero coverage, but to his right he spotted a nearby stalagmite building with a balcony and an open window. That was their only hope of escape, such as it was.

"We'll have to jump for it," he warned.

Christoffer looked over at the building and grinned. "That's more like it," he said, clapping his hands together in anticipation.

"It looks a little far," Henrik said skeptically.

The wolverines appeared at the top of the stairs, as Yorgish entered their vision on the left. He stood on the far end of the rampart, evaluating their predicament. He began advancing slowly toward them, a nasty grin on his face.

With escape so close, Aleks risked another arrow. He fired at Yorgish once, forcing the troll to duck, and shouldered the bow. Henrik slashed at the creatures behind them, and they erupted into a flurry of snarls. Christoffer shoved one into the others, and they tumbled backwards down the stairs.

"It's the only option we have. There's no time for another. Let's go!" Aleks said.

He took off running, giving himself no time to think or second-guess what he was about to do. He yelled, making a daring leap of faith at the end of the ramparts. Pin-wheeling through the air, he hit the side of the balcony with a thud. His armpits smarted from the awkward landing.

A few seconds later, Henrik landed jerkily on top of the balcony. Righting his balance, he spun and reached for Aleks' hand. Just as Aleks reached out to grab Henrik's hand, Christoffer slammed into his back. His breath escaped his lungs in a whoosh, leaving him dazed and winded. With Henrik's help, Christoffer climbed his back, and then together they grabbed him and rolled him over the edge.

He flopped for a moment like a fish, until his senses came back in a snap. He breathed in deeply and exhaled sharply. He could hear the trolls shouting to the hags to let the wolverines loose. The Wild Hunt was on again, this time with a bloodcurdling cavalcade in pursuit. He sat up, staring grimly at the commotion happening a short distance away.

"We have to keep moving. Wolverines have a keen sense of smell. There'll be no hiding from them," Henrik said.

"How do the hags get them to move in packs?" Aleks asked, standing and brushing himself off. "Aren't they normally solitary creatures?"

"It's unnatural," Henrik said, turning and slipping into the building. "They use a type of dark magic. That's why the wolverines' eyes are red. The magic also distorts the wielder."

"So that's why the hags look like scary crypt keepers," Christoffer murmured, following Henrik. He stopped just inside. "Oh, wow."

The room they were in was obviously part of a home, but it was unlike anything Aleks had ever seen. The oddly shaped and sort of circular room was undivided and looked to be solely a kitchen space. A wooden shelf lined the whole back half of the room and was piled high with precariously balanced stacks of dirty pots, pans, plates, cups, and utensils.

By the window, where the three of them stood, sat a roughhewn table. It was coated in grime and scarred heavily with knife marks. On it, next to an overturned chair, were the remnants of a meal. From under the table, a mangy, one-eyed cat meowed at them.

"We must leave here quickly," Henrik said and strode across the kitchen space, leaving a fresh trail of footprints in what was either a fine sheen of dust or dusting of flour.

Aleks and Christoffer followed. They scampered down a flight of stairs into another space. This room was a half size larger than the kitchen upstairs. A pile of wood that had been knocked over lay next to a cold fireplace. Chairs and tables were tucked into the nooks and crannies, leaving the center open for walking. A door at the end hung ajar.

"Do you think anyone lives here?" Christoffer asked, looking about.

Aleks nodded. "They must. Otherwise, why would it look like they left in a hurry?"

Christoffer picked up a discarded book and flipped it over. He read the title aloud. "*Down the Glomma: The Ogre, the Barbarian, and Me*. What is this?"

"Does it matter?" Aleks asked, rolling his eyes. "Drop it, and let's get out of here."

He did, and the three of them scurried outside and down an alleyway. Aleks knew where to go to get to the market. He took the lead and they dodged and swerved their way through the city. Wolves and wolverines howled and growled and snarled and yarled to each other, as they crisscrossed the streets, eager to pick up the scent.

Aleks didn't hesitate, he'd been on these paths before, and he nimbly managed the winding roads and tight squeezes that made up the walkways, hopping over dung left in the streets and ducking under awnings and laundry. Soon they reached a covered bridge and took refuge there, catching their breath.

Henrik stared out across the city. "We've got company coming there, there, and there," he said, pointing.

Christoffer leaned against the protective wall and groaned. "How much farther is it?"

"We're close," said Aleks, nodding in the direction they had to go.

He knew if they went a little way from the bridge, they'd be able to see the Glomma slashing across the flood plain. From that bit of knowledge, he knew that turning away from the Glomma, he'd find the market, which was closer to the center of the city.

If he could get them there, they'd be able to search for the others. Somewhere in the market with its many stalls, trolls, reindeer, bears, and wolves, were his friends and the resistance, but also danger, swift and feral and toothsome.

"When we get there, make sure nobody talks to me," said Christoffer. "I'll need to catch my breath."

Aleks clapped him on the back. "You got it," he said. "Now get moving. Break time is over."

The trio slipped from the bridge and back into the city, tripping downhill with all the haste they could muster. Aleks took them through the tall and twisted stalagmite maze. When trolls and their pets came by, they darted inside darkened thresholds. And by pets, Aleks really meant wolves.

Once, a wolf stopped, turned its head directly toward them, and snarled, sinking into a protective stance. The female troll with it followed its gaze to them, and Aleks knew they'd been spotted. The troll looked them over then glanced back over her shoulder at the sounds of an advancing squadron of wolverines. Without saying a word, she turned around, collected her wolf, and disappeared around the corner.

"We were lucky," Henrik said, watching her go.

"Yes," said Aleks, leaving their hiding spot.

"Resistance?" asked Christoffer.

"More likely she's a sympathizer," Henrik said. "Or she would have actively helped us."

As they pressed closer to the market, Aleks was forced to take them on a circuitous route, zigzagging and doubling back to avoid further detection. They evaded wolverines, hags, and palace guards. At some point, Aleks began to be grateful for their roundabout journey, because it confused the wolverines and make the hags biting mad. They shouted often, giving away their positions, so that the trio could avoid them entirely and without much effort.

All at once, Aleks felt an urge to press toward the market. Heeding it, he cut through the center streets, and they popped out into the open market. It was abuzz with tension. Furtive glances were cast their way, but like the female troll, most ignored them. A few stared sharply, their gazes a mix of interest and unfriendliness. Aleks kept a wary eye out for trouble.

Christoffer grinned and spun in a circle, drawing further attention to the three of them. "Look at this place," he said, enthusiasm evident in his tone and gaze. "What I wouldn't give to have some troll money and the time to spend it. This place is so cool. Do you see that? Is it a game?"

"Don't draw attention," Henrik chided, pushing Christoffer's hand down. "We're already too conspicuous, as it is."

"Attention? Me? Conspicuous? Us? We are the only non-trolls here. We were conspicuous to begin with," Christoffer said, rolling his eyes.

"That's what I said," Henrik said, shooting Aleks a confused look.

"You're no fun," Christoffer complained. "We'll just have to plan a weekend trip once all this is over."

"Don't count on it," said Aleks, as he cast his gaze around for signs of the resistance.

Strong hands pulled him backwards. He yelped, struggling with his captor. A hand clamped down on his mouth just as he was shouting a warning to his friends. They too were captured and dragged unceremoniously into the building.

"Quiet," a troll growled in his ear. "We're taking you to your friends."

Aleks ceased struggling and nodded. The hand slowly eased from his mouth. He turned to see his captor. He found a broad-shouldered, heavy-fisted troll with a squashed face, like it had been used for punching practice often and from an early age.

"Who are you?" he asked.

"Krog of the mighty Hammer-Fisted Rock Smashers House. You saved my son; their daughters." He pointed to himself and to the other two trolls with him. "Introduction's over. It's not safe. Come."

A lumbering female troll from Krog's trolden dropped a small, wrapped parcel. It exploded with a soft *pfft* sending out a gag-inducing cloud of mist.

"What's that?" asked Christoffer, covering his nose to block the horrible smell.

"What we need to put a wolf off its scent," Krog said, leading them further into the building.

"Or a wolverine," the female troll said.

They went through a space like a large pub, filled with endless round tables and chairs. It was circular to a point, just like the troll home had been. Krog led them behind the bar and lifted up a ratty old runner, revealing a hidden trap door. He yanked it open. The interior was dark and a scrabbling noise greeted them.

"Down," he said, his voice brooking no argument.

Aleks dropped first, fearing rats. In the distance a thin, dim line of light beckoned. Christoffer and Henrik dropped beside him. The trolls came down last. The floor shook a little, as they landed with one heavy thud after another.

Krog elbowed his way past them and led them through a short tunnel. Aleks kept a hand on the wall to keep himself oriented and upright, as Krog blocked all the light. They emerged into a dimly lit space, crammed with trolls. In the center of the tight circle Aleks saw their friends.

"You have to rescue him. They were starving him," Zaria said, plaintively. "He was eating the iron in his cell. Iron."

"He's an Iron-Bellied Stone Eater," Kanutte said, as if this explained everything. "All our kings, as far back as anyone's memory can go, have been Iron-Bellied Stone Eaters. They have a connection to the mountains. We rely on them to maintain our homes and cities."

"Is his magic from eating iron?" Aleks asked, alerting everyone to their presence. "If so, why don't all of you eat iron?"

"Aleks," cried Zaria, flinging herself into a hug. He caught her and squeezed back. She moved to Christoffer and Henrik, treating each to the same. "You're here! You're safe. Look! They were able to get some of our stuff back."

"The mirror?" Henrik asked. She shook her head no. "That's unfortunate."

She said, "We got back the Gjallarhorn, though."

"That's good, then," said Henrik.

It was a relief to be in a safe spot, or as safe as one could be amongst a small horde of mountain-trolls. Aleks and his friends managed to rest, getting some shuteye by settling in between the bigger bodies. They propped up against each other, their stuff, and the walls like a pile of puppies. Filip lapsed into snoring almost at once. The world faded, and Aleks slipped into dreamland.

It wasn't until loud voices penetrated the fog of his dreams that he stirred. Reluctantly, he woke up long before he was ready. Sitting up, he stretched out the kinks in his shoulders and yawned. He rubbed his eyes and stared at the room and its inhabitants blearily. He nudged Filip and the others awake.

"Jorkden will soon call to action the whole city to the Wild Hunt," Krog grunted from his seat on a squat stool. He passed out wrapped parcels to various trolls in the room. "When he does, everyone will have to answer the call – resistance and sympathizers alike."

The packages were opened eagerly and their contents devoured. One troll with blonde curls and a fat nose asked, "How did the supply run go?"

Krog opened his parcel and broke off some pieces of bread for Aleks and his friends. He said, "The hags and their wolverines almost caught us this time. We threw them off the trail with another scent blocker. We have to get these kids, troll and human, out of here. We won't fool the wolverines on the next pass."

"How?" asked Grizzle, an old female troll with a hoary chin. She burped and backhanded her mouth, before wiping it on her dress. "All the ways out of the city have been blocked for ages."

The trolls debated hotly on what to do, with the teenage trolls weighing in. They argued the merits of one route over another. They grew louder and louder, trying to drown out dissenting voices. Shoving broke out, and Filip hauled Zaria to safety, out of the way of flying elbows and mean punches.

"I know a way," Aleks said, pitching his voice above the din.

They ignored him.

"You'll have to shout," Zaria said.

"I know a way!" he shouted.

"Louder," Zaria urged.

He yelled, "I KNOW A WAY!"

The fighting and bickering stopped. Kanutte let go of Zorka's hair. Regnor released Modolf from a choke-hold. Falkor helped Gisken from the floor. Krog cleared his throat and righted his opponent, the blonde with the big nose. Slowly, one by one, the trolls righted themselves and retook their seats.

"Well, what is it?" Kanutte demanded impatiently.

"The Glomma," answered Aleks. "It's our escape route once again."

"That's ridiculous," Falkor said. "There's no way you could make it, even with our help. Also, it's wet."

"Rivers normally are, seeing that they're made of water and all," Christoffer said dryly, quirking an eyebrow.

"I mean it's not frozen," said Falkor.

Krog nodded. "We have no boats, and the river is forbidden to us because of the Dragomir Treaty. There's no way you can take it out of Trolgar."

"We have safe passage on it," said Zaria. She waved her hands. "Plus, I can whip up some boats."

"What do we have to lose?" asked Geirr, taking to the idea.

"Your lives," Kanutte said dryly. She smiled wickedly, her tusks menacing. "All right. I'm in."

Geirr didn't look too assured after that.

Chapter Ten: The Hunt Is On

Aleks, his friends, and the resistance emerged from their secret meeting spot into a back alley somewhere near the market. The city vibrated with tension and fear. The war horn blasted loud and long, calling all of Trolgar to action. The adult trolls froze in place. Various grimaces and scowls punctuated their faces. The horn blew again, followed by dozens and dozens of howls and yips.

"The Wild Hunt calls the whole city," Krog said, looking up and around. "We have to join or Jorkden will notice. We can't afford for the kids to be found."

"Which kids?" Filip asked. "Us or them?"

Kanutte bared her teeth at him.

Krog cracked his knuckles and said, "Both."

"We can lead them the wrong way," Grizzle said. She cast a dark look at the others. "The human children will be on their own, though."

"We can take them," offered Regnor. "Let us help."

"We just got you back. No," Krog said.

"They're not a bunch of fragile Daisy Pushers," said Grizzle, spitting on the ground.

"They need to go to the other safe house," Krog said. "We took the youngsters there earlier. We need these brutes to keep the little devils in check."

"They're Trolgar's firstborns, not babysitters," Grizzle countered, hands on hips. "Let them prove themselves. It's high time they did anyway."

"Fine," Krog conceded, grumpily. "If only to get us moving along. We're too exposed here."

"A Bow-Legged Nose Basher should lead," Grizzle said. She flashed her teeth and pushed Falkor toward Aleks. "They have the best strategies. Falkor, godson, you're in charge. Don't mess it up."

The adults left and Christoffer asked in a loud whisper, "Bow-Legged?" His lips twitched and he held back a snicker.

"Better than a Daisy Pusher, apparently," Filip whispered back.

Falkor cleared his throat and began to direct them. "I want everyone to organize into pairs. One human and one troll in each pair. This way if one of Jorkden's trolden is watching, it will always appear that a troll is in pursuit of one of you."

Geirr's mouth twisted down. "Great," he said, but he didn't really mean it.

Aleks and Zorka were paired together. Then Zaria and Kanutte. Zaria did not look happy with that at all. Kanutte on the other hand was practically gleeful. Aleks felt bad for her, but this wasn't the time to alter plans. Gisken paired with Henrik, Modolf with Geirr, then Regnor with Christoffer. That left Falkor and Filip. When everyone was matched, it was time to go.

Falkor sent the pairs off, starting with Zaria and Kanutte. Aleks watched as Kanutte followed Zaria, keeping on her heels and barking at her to "Move it!" like an army sergeant. She pushed Zaria to the left, and then they were gone from sight.

Aleks didn't know who he should pray for. The two of them were a volatile match. He wasn't sure they would get to the rendezvous point safely. Would Kanutte hurt Zaria or would she be the one in danger from the sorceress?

He didn't have time to think about it, as Falkor signaled for Zorka and him to go next. She pushed him, and he took off jogging, keeping an easy lope. He checked twice to see if Zorka was keeping up. When he looked the second time, she snarled at him.

"Eyes up front, Changeling," she said. "This is supposed to be a chase."

Aleks snapped forward and didn't look behind him again, trusting her to stick with him. He wended his way through the city, dodging the various factions of the Wild Hunt. When a group of wolves ventured too close, Zorka called out a warning.

He dodged and leapt over the back of one, startling it. The wolf turned to chase, keeping pace with Zorka, snarling and snapping after Aleks' ankles, until she whistled at it. It hesitated and she whistled again, more sharply. The wolf slowed down from a sprint to a trot and eventually stopped, but its lips twitched in agitation at giving up the hunt.

Zorka had to do that twice more when Aleks ran headlong into one of the free-roaming packs. His heart beat thickly in his throat at the near misses. He breathed out through his mouth, trying to slow its rhythmic *thump, thump, thump*.

They were close. The city's edge was near, but as the stalagmite buildings grew further and further apart, the danger increased, because they became more visible to those searching for them. The river appeared ahead of them, and Aleks surged forward leaving the safety of the buildings.

"We're lucky Jorkden smashed all the mirrors," Zorka said, coming into step with him. "Or we'd be caught under their spotlights."

Aleks looked above at the sunlight coming into the cave. Without the mirrors, it was stuck on the ceiling and diffused itself the further down it came, until it was only a dim outline of its radiance.

The river's babbling flow reached them, creating a white noise that dampened the sound of their feet on the loamy ground. Behind them the city was noisy from the crisscrossing sounds of the Wild Hunt. Barks, bays, bellows, bells, bumps, and bangs floated overhead from it, as they ran headlong for the Glomma and the safety Olaf's magic offered them as the river's guardian.

Two figures appeared out of the gloom, – Zaria and Kanutte! They were arguing at the river's edge and looked close to blows. Aleks put on a burst of speed hoping to stop them from reaching that point. Zaria turned toward the sound of his approach just as Kanutte's arm wound up for a punch.

"Look out!" Aleks shouted, but it was too late, for the troll had side-clocked her.

Zaria crumpled toward the ground. He leapt forward, catching her. They landed awkwardly with all their weight on his side. He set Zaria gently down and stood up, fury fueling him.

"What the hell?" he said, chewing out his words like he was spitting nails. "Why did you do that?"

"She had it coming," Kanutte said, unfazed.

"You're twice her size!" Aleks shouted.

"She has magic," Kanutte said, as if that made her actions acceptable.

"It wasn't a fair fight," Aleks said, shoving at her. She didn't budge, which infuriated him further. He stood back, folding his arms across his chest, and glared. "You don't hit someone when they aren't looking. It's unfair sportsmanship."

"That was wrong of you," Zorka said, staring Kanutte down. "She was their ticket out of here. How are they to get boats now?"

Kanutte shrugged, totally blasé about it. "How should I know? Besides, she needed toughening up. No Princess worth her salt would be such a prissy. And anyway, her magic is nothing but a bunch of frou-frou nonsense."

Aleks' hands dropped to his sides and curled into fists. "You're supposed to be on our side. We saved you from the banshees."

"I would have saved myself," she said defensively.

"You were turning to stone," Aleks said, amazed and appalled. He threw his hands up in the air. "How could you have saved yourself?"

Zorka narrowed her eyes to slits. "Maybe you're an inside troll. Tell me Kanutte, are you really working for Jorkden and his Wild Hunt?"

Kanutte hissed, whipping her tail around to catch Zorka by the throat, catching her by surprise. She pulled the rainbow-haired troll toward her. "Repeat that again, you Long-Eared –"

"Knottie, let her go," Falkor said, his words like ice.

He appeared out of the shadows over Zorka's shoulder, his face like a storm. She snarled at him, but Falkor snarled back louder, and beat his chest with fists the size of dinner plates. Kanutte released Zorka, and the girl shoved her away. They stumbled apart.

Filip came up just then, huffing and puffing. He took one look at Zaria, his gaze perplexed as he registered what his eyes were telling him. Crying out, he raced over and fell to his knees beside her.

"What happened?" he asked Aleks, his voice raw with worry. "Is she okay?"

Filip picked Zaria up and dragged her into his lap. Gently, he cradled her head, running a thumb lightly over a bruise that formed across her temple and jaw.

"Did someone hit her?" he asked.

Aleks nodded angrily at Kanutte. "She clocked her, just as we showed up."

Filip's nostrils flared. He turned around and stared the troll down, his jaw clenched. "Did she say why?" he asked in a deceptively even tone.

"Not really," Aleks said, feeling his temper sizzle and rise again. "Did you see the others?"

Filip looked back toward the troll city. "Christoffer and Regnor were up in the air, hurdling over balconies. We ran past them from the ground."

Aleks' eyebrows rose. "Hurdling over balconies? What were they thinking to be up there?"

Filip shrugged, careful not to disturb the unconscious girl in his arms. "I don't know. We managed to sneak out of the city because Grizzle told a group of super hairy trolls that we'd gone the other way."

"The Wooly Backs," said a new voice. It was Gisken. She was carrying Henrik over her shoulders. "We saw them, too. The Stag Lord, here, caused a distraction by throwing a crate against the wall, allowing us to lose them just before crossing the bridge."

Falkor came over to greet them. He cast a concerned look at Henrik. "Why are you carrying him?"

Her smile was teasing and full of teeth. "Because he tripped crossing the bridge."

Henrik nodded sheepishly, thanking Gisken as she sat him down. "I swear that plank came out of nowhere."

He hopped on one foot to a nearby rock and sat down with a sigh. He stretched, groaning in delight as he popped and cracked all over.

"Hey guys," Christoffer greeted, showing up with Regnor at the back of the group. "Yo, what's wrong with Zaria? What happened?"

"Knottie hit her," Falkor said. He still looked annoyed. "How is she?"

"Knottie hit her?" asked Christoffer, crouching down beside Filip. He touched Zaria's bruised cheek. "How long has she been out?"

"Just a few minutes," said Aleks. "Why aren't you mad about it?"

Christoffer gave him an offended look. "I am mad. Furious, even, but right now Zaria is more important than beating up an overgrown, gutless troll."

"Ha!" snorted Kanutte. "Fat chance! And don't call me Knottie… or gutless. Say either again, I'll string you up by your innards."

Regnor looked at Zaria with concern. He said, "Kanutte and the princess were always going to come to blows. It was only a matter of time. They get on each other's nerves."

"That's no excuse for a Black-Tailed Ribcage Butcher. How will you ever serve in the king's guard with that temper?" Falkor asked, his gaze boring a hole in Kanutte's forehead. "You know I am going to have to tell your mother."

Kanutte's eyes widened in alarm. It was the first hint of unease to cross her face. "It was only a teeny tiny punch. What's the fuss all about?"

Zaria groaned, catching everyone's attention. Filip touched her temple. "How are you feeling?"

"Like I got punched in the face," Zaria said with another low groan. She sat up and touched her jaw. She scowled at Kanutte. "You only landed that punch, because I wasn't looking."

"You punched her when she wasn't facing you?" Falkor couldn't contain his disbelief. "Are you some sort of coward? Couldn't beat up a tiny little human girl without an unfair advantage?"

"I'm not tiny," protested Zaria, standing up with Filip's help.

"Falkor, it wasn't like that," Kanutte said, stretching out a pleading hand toward him.

"Save it, Knottie. Your mother is definitely going to hear about this," he said, his lips curled in disgust.

Kanutte colored, and tightly clenched her fists. The look she gave Zaria clearly said she'd clock her again. Aleks and Christoffer positioned themselves in front of Zaria, blocking the troll's view. Even Henrik hopped over, wobbling on one foot. Aleks clamped his jaw tight to keep from saying something that would make the situation worse.

All at once the tension between them and the furious troll diffused, broken by Zorka's long ears twitching and Gisken's snickering. They doubled over laughing. At first Aleks was offended, thinking they were making fun of their show of solidarity, but both were clearly amused by Kanutte's deepening flush.

"What's so funny?" demanded Christoffer hotly.

"Knottie's mother is the head of the resistance," Regnor said.

"And our teacher when school is in session," added Gisken. She laughed so hard, she had to wipe tears from her face.

"She is one scary broad. You wouldn't want detention with her," Zorka said, grabbing her ears to stop their twitching. "Don't worry, the princess will be avenged. Kanutte will wish she had a do-over before you even reach the elves."

"Remember that time when Falkor and Modolf released pigs in the school?" Regnor asked.

Gisken smirked. "They labeled them One, Three, and Four. Everyone spent hours looking for Two."

Falkor grinned. "Your mother had my hide for that. Speaking of the devil, there's Modolf and your other little friend now."

Modolf and Geirr approached slowly, each one holding the other upright. Modolf cradled his arm and shuffle-stepped forward. Geirr's shirt was torn in several places, and he had red claw marks all over his arms and legs.

"You look like a wolverine's scratching post," Christoffer said, reaching out a hand to help.

"I was," Geirr said, accepting the support. "One of them cornered me. It was my own fault. I went the wrong way, and we got separated."

"I didn't have to wrestle the damn thing though," Modolf said, grimacing as his arm shifted. He held it closer to his body. "That was my fault. Frightened the thing, and he just started biting and scratching at everything in sight."

Pulling bandages out of his bag, Aleks hurried over to help wrap the troll's arm. Modolf consented, and Aleks had him bandaged in a jiffy. He touched the edges of a wound on the troll's shoulder.

"You might want to get that bite checked out," he told the troll.

Modolf shook his head. "Gisken digs scars. I think it will look quite dashing."

Aleks arched an eyebrow. "If you say so," he said.

The reunion halted as a fresh horn blast echoed through the wide cave. Aleks glanced up and saw a small party crest the city's hill. They were spotted.

"Time for all of us to get moving," Falkor said. "We need to get back to the city and to our next safe house. Princess, you'd best be creating those boats right about now."

Zaria went to the river's edge. She held out her hands like she was holding a ball of fire and widened the gap. The ruse looked much more convincing this time. A wooden boat appeared, dropping from the sky and splashing those who stood nearby.

Filip wiped water from his face just as a second boat plopped down. He gave her a self-deprecating grin and wiped off again. When it happened a third time, he stepped away, laughing and saying, "Zar-Zar. I think I'm wet enough now."

She flicked her fingers at him and another splash of water rose up from the river and hit him square between the eyes. She smirked at his pouting expression and sent a wave of warm air his way. Aleks shared a grin with Christoffer. Things seemed to be looking up for their blond friend in the love department. About time.

"Thanks, Zar-Zar," Filip said, shaking droplets out of his hair and wiggling a finger in his ear to clear it out. "You might want to make oars, too, just in case we need to row or something."

"Good thinking," she said and pointed at the boats in turn, conjuring up a set of oars for each. The first set looked lopsided.

"Everyone should get on board," Aleks said, grabbing a long rope from his bag. He looped it around the stern of one boat and the bow of the other, connecting them. "We should tie all three together. Anybody have another rope?"

"I've got one," Geirr said, reaching into his bag. "It's a good thing the resistance got our stuff back."

"Well most of it," said Filip. "I'm down to one bag."

Aleks took the rope from Geirr and connected the last boat to the others. "Now we won't get separated in the dark."

Christoffer and Filip took the last boat, loading it with their bags. Henrik and Geirr took the middle boat, leaving Aleks and Zaria to take the lead boat. Their spotters, realizing that the trolls with them weren't capturing them, blasted the horn, alerting the Wild Hunt that the chase was on.

Regnor shook Zaria's hand. "My uncle wants me to give you his thanks. He'd be here, but he's with a group of highly trusted trolls surrounding Jorkden and can't risk being seen."

"Who's your uncle?" asked Filip, grabbing his oar and putting it in the water.

"Yorgish," Regnor said, helping Zaria take her seat. He braced his hands on the boat, stopping their wayward drifting. "He was the black sheep of the family for a long time."

"Yorgish? Really? I would never have guessed it. He seems like other trolls to me. What exactly did he do?" asked Zaria.

Regnor leaned in conspiratorially, whispering, "He did some things that the head of the family didn't approve of – getting friendly with an elf, I think, – so they barred him from the house. Now, he's the hero of the family. Most likely he'll be voted in as the new head, after all this is over. They're treating him like he is even now."

"How do you know you can trust him? Wouldn't it be more likely that he'd sabotage the resistance?" asked Aleks. He finished securing their bags and grabbed his oar, sliding it into the water.

Regnor shook his head. "He's been feeding information to Morvin, who then brings it to us to act on. Neither he nor Morvin are told anything about what we do until after the wheels have been set in motion. Plausible deniability and genuine reactions are key to keeping all of our heads where they should be – on our necks."

"That's wise," Zaria said. "This way they can't carry information back to Jorkden by fair means or foul."

"We should launch them. The Wild Hunt is coming," Falkor said, as he stood sentinel nearby, every inch the leader, watching the city behind them.

The din of the Wild Hunt reached them before the sight of the horde crested the city's last hill. Falkor, Regnor, and Zorka pushed the boats out into the river where the current could pick them up. They were careful to avoid stepping into the Glomma, knowing that Olaf, would have their hides if they tried to use it.

As they drifted away, Aleks had a thought. He turned around to the trolls on the shore. "Try to find that mirror we had. Use it to keep in touch with us. Try to contact the dwarves for King Flein's aid."

"What does the mirror look like?" asked Gisken.

"Handheld, dark silver, with flowers," Christoffer said, cutting off Zaria's more elaborate description of antiqued silver with delicate floral filigree.

"We'll find it," promised Regnor. "Once we have it, how does it work?"

"There's a mechanism in the handle. Click it and say the name of who you want to contact," Filip said, waving. "Thanks for getting us out."

"Our debt is paid," Falkor said, waving back. "You saved us. We've saved you. Our help ends here."

"The Wild Hunt is upon us," Kanutte said. "We should go, before we're captured for aiding the humans."

"Good luck to you all," Modolf said, readjusting his bandages as he prepared to take off. "You'll need it."

Chapter Eleven: Glomma Drama

As wolves bayed in the dark, the three little boats picked up speed. Together, the six of them used the oars to propel themselves forward, sluicing steadily through the waters. Deep into the cave they went, silent as church mice, all aware of the danger following them, baying at their heels.

Aleks looked back once to watch as their helpers disappeared into the murky gloom. The teenage trolls merged into the shadows, melding within the chaos of the Wild Hunt as if they'd been there all along. Falkor howled, and the war cry jerked Aleks back to his senses. He whipped forward and paddled harder.

He and his friends were left to face what lay ahead on their own. Aleks had to hope that they could reach Álfheim before the Wild Hunt got them. It was their only chance to escape and the only way to freedom that he could see.

Knowing that distance meant safety, Aleks urged Zaria to press onward. They led the others on the river. As the pack fell further behind them, Aleks was tempted to use the stargazer to help light their path, but he didn't want to tax the thing further. This was its third time out of the house and Aleks needed it to last through the end of their adventure.

He tapped Zaria on the shoulder. "Can you do anything to help us see?" he asked.

"Is it safe?" she asked in a low whisper.

He nodded, and then realizing she couldn't really see him, said, "Yes."

Zaria conjured up a small lantern and stuck it to the front of the boat, illumining the dark waters. The yellow glow of light was hemmed in on all sides. They strained to see beyond the shallow light that was cast. In the gloom there was nothing to see but shifting shadows flitting here and there like veiled threats.

Relief from the oppressive darkness came infrequently from small holes high above. Sunlight faintly trickled down, lighting their way as if they were boating under the stars. It was magical, like sailing under their own private Milky Way.

As the noise of the Wild Hunt faded into echoes, Aleks hoped Falkor and the others would make it to their next safe house. He hoped Kanutte would get her comeuppance, and he hoped the resistance would find the mirror and free Kafirr. Part of him couldn't believe he hoped Kafirr was back in power, but compared to Jorkden the Iron-Bellied Stone Eater was a saint.

"Zar-Zar, Do you suppose you could whip us up something to eat? I'm famished," Filip called out from the last boat.

"My stomach's rumbling, too," Aleks said. "Maybe we should eat."

"I fight off wolverines much better on a full stomach," added Geirr, joining the attempt to wheedle delicious treats from the sorceress.

"I'll send something back," Zaria promised.

Moments later thuds and splashes hailed the arrival of a feast. Items fell without rhyme or reason into the boats, knocking against the boats, bouncing off heads and bodies, and hitting the water. Aleks reached out and caught a plum as it hurtled headlong toward the river. He took a bite out of it, letting the juices run down his hand and chin.

Zaria looked on with dismay, watching as several things sank below the surface. "So much waste. I need to work on my aim. This is dreadful."

"We're moving," Aleks said, consoling her. He finished off the plum, tossing the pit. "I'm sure that makes a difference. It's not like we're picnicking with a blanket and staying in one spot."

"Nevertheless, something needs to be done about it, or all our food will be on the bottom of the Glomma," she said, propping the oar across her knees. She held out her hands and a plate of sandwiches appeared.

As she passed him the plate, he stopped oaring, too. Henrik and Geirr's boat caught up. Aleks could see that Geirr was chowing down on a turkey leg. He gave them a thumbs up. Henrik reached over the gap between their boats and took the plate from him and began scarfing down the sandwiches one after another, eating them in as little as two bites.

Filip and Christoffer slid beside them on the other side. The movement caused the three boats to knock softly together. Aleks took another plate of sandwiches from Zaria and passed it over. Filip and

Christoffer grabbed one for each hand. Zaria handed him a third plate, and Aleks gratefully stuffed his face.

There were ham and cheese sandwiches; tuna salad, peanut butter and jelly, turkey club — and that was only the first layer. Aleks easily ate one of each and greedily eyed the second layer. Zaria plucked a chicken salad sandwich and sank her teeth into it.

The Wild Hunt was a distant memory. The wolves, wolverines, and horns had long faded. Nothing snuffled in the dark. Bobbing quietly in place, their way lit by the single lantern, they ate until they almost popped. Zaria provided chips, sodas, cookies, and at the end when they couldn't take another bite, supplied everyone with water bottles.

Christoffer sighed contentedly. "Oh man, that was amazing. I'm sleepy. Can we rest? We've been up for ages and that nap earlier hardly counts."

"What do you think?" Aleks asked Henrik. "Is it safe to rest? We can take turns keeping a watch."

Henrik eyed the way they'd come. "I don't know," he said, a worried frown pulling his eyebrows down. "If we made it to Álfheim, I'd feel better."

Zaria yawned, barely able to contain it with her hand. She blinked at them sleepily. "I vote we all rest. We're tied together. What's the worst that could happen?

We drift to shore? If the boat hits the ground, we'd feel it and wake up."

"The river runs really close to the edge of the cave at this section. The worst thing that could happen is we strike the walls and sink," Henrik said.

"I'm too tired to think straight," Geirr said, taking the opportunity to lie out, resting his head against his bag. "I could sleep for a whole month of Sundays."

"I think that settles it," said Filip, copying Geirr and propping himself against the seat, using his backpack as a headrest. "It's time for some shut-eye."

"You can rest, Zaria," Aleks offered. "Henrik, Christoffer, and I will keep the boats moving and we can switch off later."

It was hard to see Christoffer's face, shrouded as it was in shadows, but he sounded put upon as he said, "What? How did I manage to get first shift? This was my suggestion. Uncool. Wake up, Filip."

"I can't hear you," Filip singsonged, rolling over. "Night, night."

"He is totally grinning, the cheeky buzzard," Christoffer said, complaining; but he picked up his oar and took up position. "Rude, so rude."

Filip laughed softly as Aleks helped Zaria settle into the bottom of their boat. She curled up into a loose ball, pressing her face into a sweater-turned-pillow. He looked at Henrik and nodded. The two launched their boats forward one by one with Christoffer keeping up the rear.

With half of the group sleeping, all was quiet, punctuated only by Filip's outrageous snores. They sawed through the air and winged up to the stalactites hanging from the cave's ceiling. The sound of fluttering and chittering drew Aleks' gaze upward. Glowing eyes peered back at him.

"Bats," said Henrik, following his gaze. "We've got company."

"It's not the worst company we've had," Aleks joked.

"No, but this company might poop on you," Henrik said, pulling his cloak lower over his head.

Aleks brushed the top of his head feeling for phantom bat droppings. He picked up speed, drawing the boats away from the danger zone. Henrik laughed and pulled his oar harder through the water. There was a bit of drag resistance that he hadn't noticed before. When Aleks looked over his shoulder, he saw Christoffer slumped over his oar, asleep. He shook his head, bemused, and turned back in time to guide them around a bend.

The river flowed strongly now. The current pushed and pulled on their boats. As the lead, it was up to

Aleks to spot the eddies that signaled rocks in the water. He and Henrik took turns using their oars to push the boats away from the rocks and their imminent danger to the boats. It took some work to protect the last boat, but they could manage. They just had to be extra careful.

"We're close now," Henrik said. He grunted at the effort to move his and Geirr's boat around another group of rocks.

"I know," said Aleks, watching Henrik prod Filip's and Christoffer's boat out of the way. "We should pull to shore around the next bend."

They pushed free and Aleks turned around and pulled his oar through the water. They'd barely moved when a sickening crack sounded followed by a violent jolt. Aleks nearly toppled over the edge of his boat. Their progress came to a full-on stop. They were dead in the water. He stood cautiously and leaned over the front of the boat, using the lantern to peer straight down.

Aleks swallowed hard, dread sliding down his gullet. "Damn," he hissed.

"You weren't looking," Henrik said, reproachfully. "You're the navigator."

"I know, I know, and I'm sorry," said Aleks. He was angry at himself for being so careless.

He bent over to shake Zaria awake. He needn't have bothered, because she awoke at the touch of the chilled water seeping into the bottom of the boat. She stared at him blearily, a frown marring her face. Confused, she looked around and down. Her fingers swished in the water uncomprehendingly.

"There's water in the boat," she said.

"Yes," said Aleks, grabbing her by her armpits and hauling her upright. "We need to transfer boats."

The water was already swirling around his ankles. Henrik moved his boat closer, careful to keep it away from the rocks that had wrecked their boat. He reached out to grab her and Aleks transferred Zaria's weight to his arms. The boats wobbled dangerously under their shifting weights.

"Got her," said Henrik. "Go get your bags."

The water was halfway up his calves. Their bags were soaked through and heavy. He swung his waterlogged backpack over his shoulder, grabbed hers in his other hand, and used his oar to drag Christoffer's and Filip's boat to him.

He tossed Zaria's bag, hitting Christoffer square in the chest, startling him awake. He caught it on reflex and Aleks tossed him his next, before readying himself to follow. The water swirled by his knees, the boat almost completely submerged at this point.

"What's going on?" Christoffer asked around a jaw-cracking yawn. "Why are you tossing me your bags? And why are they soaking wet?"

"Budge over," said Aleks, planting his foot in the boat. "I'm coming on board."

Christoffer sidled over, giving him space. "I can see that, but why are you coming over here?"

"We lost the front boat," Aleks said grimly. "It's my fault. I was stupid."

"That's not unusual," said Christoffer, trying to inject some humor. Filip had yet to stir.

Aleks pressed his lips into a tight line. "I wasn't paying attention, and I missed the rocks."

Christoffer looked over and saw the sunken boat. It was nearly filled to the brim and barely floated under the heavy load weighing it down. The lantern snuffed out, making it difficult to see anything. Aleks caught a glimmer of light from the corner of his eye as it bounced off Henrik's sword when the Stag Lord used it to cut the rope tying his boat to the lead boat. With the connection severed, the middle boat was now the lead boat, and three were now two.

"Five more minutes," Filip grumbled, shifting positions.

"The water is low," said Henrik. "That's why all the rocks are exposed."

"Why is it so low?" asked Zaria, accepting an oar from Henrik. She was alert now.

Henrik grabbed the other oar and sat down. "Olaf agreed not to flood Trolgar under the revised Dragomir Treaty."

"So he's decreased its flow?" she asked.

"It appears that way. I could use some light, Princess," he said.

"We could use another boat," said Christoffer.

"This is easier," said Zaria, holding out her hands for a lantern. She tipped her head to the fast flowing currents racing by them. "Plus, a boat might float away before we can secure it."

A second later a new lantern appeared, and she passed it forward. Henrik secured it to the prow of the boat. Her magic was dead useful at times, unlike his. Aleks sighed gustily. Why did it feel like he couldn't even navigate his way out of a paper bag?

"Don't beat yourself up," said Christoffer, as if reading his thoughts. "It could have happened to any one of us."

Aleks knew that, but it wasn't supposed to happen to him. He always knew the right way to go. He always knew how to get around obstacles. So this just didn't sit right with him. The whole situation was messed up. It shouldn't be happening. Not yet. Not until his majority.

He still had more time, didn't he? His fey gifts should work until then, shouldn't they? What had Kafirr said? He could barely think straight. He felt like a connection he'd taken for granted had been cut and was now hanging by a thread ready to snap at a moment's notice.

Geirr sat up between Zaria and Henrik. He looked at her confused and then peered over the edge of the boat. He let out a low whistle. "Damn. That boat is toast. You're lucky you didn't completely capsize."

Christoffer kicked Filip's feet. "Wake up you loggerhead. Your snoring sunk a boat."

"What?" he asked, squinting at him and Aleks. "That's impossible." He shielded his face from the light. "Why are you in this boat?"

"Because you sunk a boat with your snoring," Christoffer repeated, repressing a smirk. "Take a look, and see for yourself."

He leaned back and waved a hand in invitation. Filip sat up, his mouth agape, for he saw the boat bobbing drunkenly a short distance away. As they watched, the boat disappeared from view, finding a home on the bottom of Olaf's river.

"I hit a rock," explained Aleks when Filip turned back to look at them.

"Must have been some rock," Filip deadpanned.

Henrik cleared his throat, calling everyone's attention. He gestured ahead of them. "We don't have far. If we can get around the next bend and to the shore, we'll be close to Master Brown's."

"Let's get going then," said Christoffer. He handed his oar to Filip. "Your turn."

A short laugh escaped Aleks. "You fell asleep. I think it's still your turn." He handed Christoffer his oar.

Christoffer stuck out his tongue, but took it. Aleks rested his elbows on his knees and stared at the slick cave walls and into the dark swirling water. Ostensibly he was looking for rocks, same as Geirr, but what Aleks really searched for was his fey magic.

It had been a part of him for so long, it was hard to believe it wasn't there now. He touched his ears. Was it his imagination or were they rounder now? He closed his eyes trying to sense the distance to Master Brown's. A flicker of recognition sparked within him.

He sighed in relief. It was one thing to want his magic to disappear, but it was another for it to happen sooner than he expected. He was counting on the magic to help him and his friends. And, it wasn't like he wanted to keep it forever, just until he was fully human. Then it could leave him.

He felt adrift, like a lonely mariner praying for dry land, for something recognizable. He felt vulnerable and weak, and he didn't like it. Not one bit. Then there was the other problem; didn't Grams say leaving home would allow him to keep his magic?

So what the heck was going on? Shouldn't it be getting stronger? Why was it getting weaker like he was losing a signal? Was there some sort of interference? Aleks didn't know, and that was a problem – a big one – because he was either losing his magic or something or someone was blocking it. Neither option was good. Both were a problem for another day.

After navigating around the bend, Henrik guided the boats to the tiny shoreline. When the bottom of the boats hit sand everyone got out, taking their things. Although there had been no signs of the Wild Hunt since they traveled down the river, it was decided that they should leave no trace of their passing behind. Zaria zapped the boats away and just like that there was nothing for the trolls to find.

They followed the cave's sloping floor toward the surface. The Glomma disappeared, following a path that now traveled away from them. The climb was tiring, but everyone pressed onward, knowing that rest would come soon. Aleks could hardly wait to take a load off his tired feet. He was bone weary and struggled to keep his eyes open. Geirr had to nudge him back into place every time he began to wander too close to the cave walls.

At last they reached a familiar spot. The illusion was still as flawless today as it had been the first time he'd seen it. The rock wall at first glance appeared to be nothing special, but it hid a secret. The wall was not nearly as solid as it looked. There was an opening that led to a hidden corridor that went to Master Brown's house. A cantankerous brownie, Master Brown was the guardian of Álfheim, and protected a mechanical elevator to the surface.

Henrik went through the opening first. It looked like he disappeared into the wall, but he was merely sliding around it. Aleks went next, and the others single-file came behind him. The sound of water echoed loudly off the walls, making it difficult to talk, so great was the roar.

A circular chamber opened up at the end of the long hallway. A natural waterfall thundered down the middle of the room, next to a metal door set into the wall. Water rushed over and through an elaborate wooden aqueduct and waterwheel. Dozens of leaky buckets on creaky ropes carried water from the pool into the air and onto the track. There, their loads tipped and splashed unsteadily before returning to pick up fresh loads of water.

Hundreds and hundreds of fireflies lit the space like strands of twinkling holiday lights. They were the only visible light source in the whole space, winking steadily on and off, on and off. Careless of the intruders, the fireflies brushed against their skins. Aleks fought the urge to bat them away, disliking the fluttering sensation.

Henrik knocked briskly on the metal door. When nobody answered for some time, he knocked again, louder. Inside, a harsh muttering rumbled; Master Brown opened the peephole and peered out. His squeaky voice rang out upon their heads.

"Not you again," he said, vexed. "For the last time, I don't help humans."

Chapter Twelve: The White Raven

"Then help me," said Henrik, stepping backward so the brownie could see his white cloak and golden antlers.

"New Stag Lord?" Master Brown asked. At his nod, the brownie's eyes narrowed shrewdly. "Can you get my favorites like Hector got for me?"

Henrik said, "I can, but only if you help all of us."

"I want double my last order," Master Brown squawked imperiously. "Yes, double, or no deal."

"You know they're hard to come by," Henrik hedged. On seeing the brownie's mutinous expression, he said, "I will try, but double is going to be difficult."

"Try?" scoffed Master Brown, his beady eyes flashing. "It's double or nothing."

"What does he want?" asked Christoffer abstractly, talking over his shoulder. He was transfixed by the water system and couldn't take his eyes off of it.

"Master Brown wants white ravens," said Henrik. "Double what my father brought him last time."

Aleks was baffled. He looked at the Stag Lord, asking, "White ravens? Not black? For what purpose? Does he use them as pets?"

"He doesn't eat them for supper, does he?" asked Geirr. He paused, considering. "Squab is good. It might taste similar?"

"I would never eat a white raven," Master Brown said, affronted. "Never."

"Where do you get them?" asked Zaria, looking between the Stag Lord and the brownie.

"If you're fortunate, in the wild. Otherwise they're bred by the witch in the woods," Henrik said, compressing his mouth into a thin line. "If they are treated properly they can bond with their owners and be trained to talk and carry messages. As rare as white ravens are, a bonded white raven is rarer still."

Aleks raised an eyebrow. "Wouldn't carrier pigeons be easier? I've even heard that owls deliver packages."

"Don't be silly, that last one is from a book," said Zaria, rolling her eyes.

"I know that," he said, rolling his eyes back at her.

Henrik stared at the brownie. "Why do you need double, when you already have five? My father brought you three the last time. He marked it down in his last notebook. Won't eleven ravens be too much to care for down here?"

Master Brown muttered something unintelligible.

"I didn't catch that," said Aleks, cupping a hand to his ear.

"I said I haven't been able to get one to talk," snapped Master Brown. "For some reason they're not bonding to me."

"It's probably not at all because he's a tetchy grouch," said Filip in an aside to Christoffer.

"You've tried unsuccessfully to bond with the other ravens. If you want a double order, wouldn't it be better to start fresh? Why don't you hand yours over to me?" asked Henrik in his most reasonable manner.

Aleks wondered if this was how Hector had sounded while negotiating.

Filip added, "Think about it, your new ravens won't learn bad manners from the others. They'll have more space and more of your attention. I bet one would bond then."

Henrik flashed Filip a thumbs-up and said, "Give me the five you have, and I'll be back with more."

"What? All five of my white ravens?" squeaked Master Brown, aghast. "No! That wasn't the deal. I refuse. I don't accept." He slammed the peephole and threw an extra lock into place for good measure.

"You don't need five untrained and unbonded white ravens," Henrik cajoled, channeling more of his father's smooth-talking ways. He rapped on the door. "You know only one will ever bond with you. Only one will take orders and messages from you. How long have you had the others? Why don't you hand them over?"

"How many white ravens are there in the world?" asked Aleks.

"Not enough to let one brownie keep eleven of them," said Henrik. "Six is stretching it. Even the witch in the woods doesn't have that many. But, now that I'm thinking about it, I might be able to get a trained one."

"Trained?" Master Brown asked through the door, derisively, but there was an expectant silence.

Henrik flashed a quick grin at them. "I heard of a giant who transformed, and his white raven is free. She stays near him even now. It is possible to capture her and bring her to you."

When a giant transforms, he becomes inert, returning to the rocks from which he emerged. The white raven Henrik talked about must be circling an inanimate mountainous crag somewhere in Jötunheim, the land of the giants. The idea saddened Aleks. He could imagine the raven's melancholy cry, as it mourned for its master as it flew, peering down at the earth waiting for him to reappear.

Henrik added, temptingly, "You'd have a head start with her because she already talks."

Master Brown opened the peephole again. "Deal," he said. "One talking raven or six untrained ones. White, of course."

"And you'll give us the other five ravens in your quarters," pressed Henrik.

Master Brown's mouth curled into a tight moue. "No," he snapped. "Don't ask again."

"We can always sing for you, like we did before," Aleks offered.

He flashed a wicked smile remembering the awful singing they had all once performed for Master Brown. Zaria was a truly atrocious singer. There was no way she could call wildlife to her with just the sound of her voice. Disney got that one wrong with this princess.

"Don't you dare!" Master Brown screeched, remembering the horrendous performance as well. "I will not tolerate that caterwauling noise you call singing. You sing, and the deal is off. I'm coming out, Hector. Keep them quiet."

The peephole slammed shut for the second time.

"It's Henrik, actually," the Stag Lord said, a tad sheepishly.

"Whatever," groused Master Brown.

In the silence, Aleks turned to Henrik. "Why are we taking his birds?"

Henrik pressed his mouth into a grim line. "Many reasons. First, it's easier to trade for a white raven if you have another to exchange. Like I said, only one will bond with you. He doesn't need to keep so many. One will do. And second, a bird shouldn't be kept underground without sunlight and space to fly."

A flurry of sounds erupted from behind the door. Metal clacked and groaned, locks snapped back, ravens cawed and croaked, and screeched and squawked. Master Brown opened the door and stepped off of a stool. At his blue, hairy, bare feet sat five mismatched antique black cages, each holding one white raven. They shuffled uneasily and clacked a warning to come no closer.

Of the five ravens, only one was white, like purest snow from the tip of its beak to the tips of its talons. It was pristine with sharp, black eyes. One looked like it had rolled around in the dirt and needed a bath, appearing more gray than white. The remaining three had slightly pink beaks and feet. Of those, one had pale blue eyes and the others had black. A smudge of gray graced the head of one of the black-eyed pink-beaked ravens like a thumbprint.

Henrik picked up two of the cages, and Aleks copied him, grabbing two more. Christoffer stopped gaping at their surroundings to pick up the last cage. The ravens made knocking sounds, which made Aleks want to say 'Nevermore,' back to them. Zaria tried to touch the snow-white bird's feathers. It snapped at her fingers, making her jump and snatch her hand back. She laughed nervously.

"I don't have all day," Master Brown said, shooing the kids toward a circle in the center of the floor. "Get to your positions."

He didn't wait for them and hurried around turning a series of switches on and off, adjusting dials and knobs, and stuck his hand on a lever.

"No flash photography is permitted. Keep your hands, feet, bird cages, and other belongings behind the railing at all times. It is ill-advised to disregard these rules. Don't come crying to me if you're injured."

"Railing?" asked Christoffer, looking around. He made a move to step off the flush platform.

Geirr hauled him back as the brownie yanked the lever down, and a railing sprang up from the floor, stopping at their waists. Christoffer grabbed it just in time as the platform zipped skyward on a rush of water. One of Aleks' birds pecked him on the shin. He cursed, but didn't let go, holding tighter onto the cage and rail.

They hurtled toward the ceiling on a geyser of water. Christoffer cried out, ducking, causing Filip to laugh. Aleks nudged Christoffer and pointed to a circular spot on the ceiling that was beginning to open. Wind whistled past his ears, and his stomach swooped unpleasantly. Their skyward thrust halted the instant they drew in line with the opening.

A familiar friend greeted them. "Hello children, it's nice to see you all again. Stag Lord welcome back. Are you on your way to Elleken? They've moved locations again."

Their new companion was an elf with large, pointy, ears. Aleks was glad not to have them. They stuck out like sore thumbs, literally, but he supposed they looked fine on the elf. Edevart had pale blond hair and a groomed mustache. He wore an old starchy style of clothing that wouldn't look out of place in a Charles Dickens' movie.

Henrik tilted his head in acknowledgement. "Edevart, you are a welcome face after the trouble we've gone through to get here. Where is Elleken these days?"

"Your godmother has shifted it closer to the edge of Gloomwood, just west of the Gjöll," Edevart said as he flipped a matching lever to Master Brown's down below. The rails swooshed back inside the platform.

"What's Elleken?" asked Geirr, getting off first.

"It's the home of the ellefolken," explained Henrik. "It's built of tents so it's mobile. We move it around Gloomwood and the Golden Kings so we can patrol the east side of the forest."

"Right, and the elves generally take the west half," said Edevart.

"How's Frida?" Zaria asked him, as the elf helped her off the platform.

"The wife is splendid, just splendid," he said, practically beaming with pride. "She's with child, about four months along."

She gave him a hug. "That's wonderful news!"

"This will be our first," he said, beaming. "I'm a touch nervous about being a father, but I can't wait to greet the little babe."

Edevart took the cages from Aleks and the others and placed them on the ground. Aleks jumped off, glad to be back on solid ground and birdless. The mechanical elevator, while cool, wasn't the safest thing to be standing on. If the water pressure fluctuated, the whole thing would plummet like a stone, taking its riders with it.

"Look at this place," said Christoffer. "This is amazing. Are those glass buildings?"

They were. Álfheim was a city built into the trees. The last time Aleks had been here, the place had been covered in snow and ice. Today it was vibrant with flowers and birdsong. The sun hung low in the sky, heavy with golden color. It dripped and drizzled over everything like honey.

Elves and ellefolken wandered about on bridges strung like glittery necklaces between the trees. Neighbors greeted neighbors, exchanging pleasantries and small gifts. In the center space between the trees a large fire pit was monitored by a gaggle of elves busy preparing for the evening's festivities.

"I don't suppose you could house us for the day and night, could you?" asked Henrik. "We are in sore need of rest and victuals."

"Of course, of course," said Edevart. "Give me a moment to shut this down and I'll take you myself. Frida will be so pleased to see you all."

"Will she make her little teacakes?" asked Filip, hopefully. "Those were great."

Edevart nodded, clapping Filip on the back as he passed, and went to call Master Brown on a low-tech phone-like device. Elves loved to incorporate human technology into their day-to-day lives, but on their terms, choosing to make everything as green as possible. Moments later the platform disappeared, and the hole closed shut. Grass hid its location so well you'd never guess by looking that a brownie lived below.

Edevart took a cage from Henrik and led them away. Aleks picked up his ravens and followed the elf toward his home. Like everyone else, Aleks looked forward to a good sleep, but his hopes were dashed twenty steps into crossing the glade.

Nori appeared out of nowhere, like a magician on a stage, only not nearly as pleasant or as entertaining.

Her hair bristled with untamed energy. Her sudden appearance discomfited him. Even the raven with him shuffled uneasily in his sister's presence. Her being here spelled trouble, and he'd had enough of it.

"Where have you been?" she demanded, placing her hands on her hips. "Did you get lost?"

Aleks quirked a disbelieving eyebrow. "You're the one who got lost. Don't you remember? We weren't even supposed to meet here, but at Jerndor."

Nori waved a hand. "Never mind, you're here now. We must speak to Queen Silje and get her help. We have no time to lose. You've wasted enough of it as it is and we need to reach Niffleheim."

Aleks moved her aside and kept walking. "Nori, we're tired. We haven't had a chance to get a good night's sleep. It can wait."

"It can't," she hissed, keeping in step with him. "Every moment you delay is another moment the dragon is left unchecked. We have to get organized."

"Go talk to Silje yourself," he said.

"I can't get an audience," Nori said, waspishly. "It's extremely rude. I'm royalty after a fashion. That alone should be reason enough for her to see me."

It was enough to send him running in the opposite direction. If only he could escape her now. He hadn't seen her for more than five minutes and already she was driving him batty. He didn't have enough sleep to deal with her today.

The sound of something like a bear trumpeting called their attention. Norwick raced across the glade.

"Come here you handsome brute," Henrik said affectionately.

He took a few jogging steps towards the winter-wyvern. Norwick pounced, tackling Henrik to the ground. The Stag Lord chuckled as the beast began to enthusiastically lick his face with a great big tongue.

Winter-wyverns were fire-breathing beasts with great leathery wings like bats. Their bodies were a cross between a bear and a large cat with long canines. They had scaly feet and came in a variety of colors. Norwick's fur reminded Aleks of a snow leopard's pattern. He was big, bold, and breathtaking, and way cooler than a horse to ride.

Henrik gave Norwick a vigorous scratching, getting behind the ears, under the chin, around the shoulders. He even got Norwick's belly when the winter-wyvern flopped over onto his side like a lazy cat. When Norwick caught sight of Zaria, he sprang to his feet and began licking her face. She giggled and petted him.

Aleks greeted the creature, too, earning a lick himself. He liked Norwick. For the chance of owning one he'd be sorely tempted to keep his magic and pointy ears. Flying on a winter-wyvern was an exhilarating experience, especially knowing it wasn't going to eat him. Otherwise, a winter-wyvern could be pretty terrifying to encounter.

He remembered his first meeting with Norwick. The winter-wyvern had gotten the best of him and Filip and snatched them up by their ankles in his claws. The flight to the cave had seemed like a trip to their doom, until Hector appeared and offered them food.

With one last affectionate pat on the beast's rump, Aleks and his friends continued to Edevart's house. They left the ravens outside on the walkway to bask in the fading sunlight, the first they'd probably enjoyed in a long time. Nori tried to persuade them to leave with her tonight, but they all ignored her. She huffed and flung herself uninvited onto one of Frida's kitchen chairs.

"Edevart told us the good news," Filip said, eagerly assisting Frida in her tea preparations. He stole a few treats as he set everything out.

"You look great," Zaria said. She closed her eyes and inhaled the steam rising from her cup. "Ah... this smells heavenly."

"Thank you, Princess," Frida said, tucking her loose braid over a shoulder. "I feel great. I like being pregnant."

She was fair, freckled, and fresh-faced. Flour and sugar coated her apron and clung to her hands. Aleks watched as her husband pressed her gently into a chair, served her tea, and arranged a small plate of cakes before her. Frida smiled at him indulgently, and the two got lost in their own little world. The moment was abruptly cut short by a snort from Nori.

Edevart cut his gaze her way. "You're Grimkell's daughter, right? Why are you here?"

Nori glared at him balefully. "I am. As for why I'm here and not in Niffleheim, well it's only a matter of life and death, not that anyone cares."

Frida hid a little smile behind a bite of cake. "Since you're here, you might as well try one of my famous teacakes. It'll do you good and take your mind off your worries."

"I must speak to Silje," Nori insisted, ignoring the cakes, passing them up with an indelicate sniff.

Aleks stole her cakes and popped them into his mouth. Zaria raised a chiding eyebrow. "What? If she doesn't want them, I do."

She flicked her gaze to Nori, then to the cakes. She gave him a conspiratorial grin. "Pass me one."

"How are things in Trolgar? They've been quiet lately. More cakes?" Frida asked. "Edevart, dear, there are more in the cupboard over there."

He stood up and got them, bringing them back to the table. Filip snatched another one.

Henrik took down his hood and rubbed his face. "It's awful down there."

Aleks nodded. "Jorkden overthrew Kafirr. There's a real power struggle happening. The Wild Hunt now comprises hags, wolverines, and banshees."

Edevart choked. Frida took his cup from him, handing it to Geirr. She patted his back, until he found his voice. "Impossible. Inconceivable. How?"

"Regrettably, possible and conceivable," Henrik said. "We rescued some of the great families' firstborns. They can now focus on leading the resistance."

"Freeing Kafirr is their first priority," said Zaria, setting aside her cakes. "He needs rescuing, but he won't die of starvation."

"Not now, at any rate," said Christoffer. "Zaria used magic to make him a small stockpile of food."

"Why didn't you rescue him?" asked Frida. "We should tell Queen Silje; Nori is right about that."

"Nori didn't know," Geirr said, finishing a cake and licking his fingers. "She wasn't with us."

"Kafirr's imprisonment, Jorkden's rule – it all has to do with Fritjof. All of it. We need to stop him," Nori said, slamming a fist on the table. "We need a plan, and we can't wait."

"Fritjof?" asked Edevart.

"Not you too," Nori complained. "Why does nobody remember he's a dragon and Koll's brother?"

The father-to-be shared a worried look with his wife. Frida shrugged, and rubbed her protruding belly. She didn't know anything either.

"I'll see that you get that meeting with our queen," said Edevart, pushing his seat back. He stopped halfway out of his chair, frowning down at them as Henrik's head weaved unsteadily. "But first, you all need some respite."

Nori, of course, protested, but she was overruled. Everyone gathered together creating makeshift nests out of sleeping bags, blankets, pillows, and cushions. They fell asleep in minutes with arms flung across eyes, hair tickling noses, knees into their neighbors' backs, and feet in each other's faces. They were too tired to care.

A raven called out, and it was the last sound anyone heard. Not even Filip's snores registered. That's why when something sharp knocked on his head hours later, Aleks woke with a start staring into shrewd beady eyes. Taken aback, he shouted, "Ahh!"

Lurching to a sitting position he frantically swiped at the creature. The white raven retorted angrily, screeching, "Eye-riii!" It flew off in a flurry of feathers to sit on the back of a kitchen chair. Its icy blue stare a cold reproach.

Chapter Thirteen:
Flight to Jerndor

Aleks stood and stalked menacingly toward the raven. "How did you get out?"

It ca-cawed at him and Aleks imagined that it sounded like 'blockhead.' He looked over at his friends as they struggled to wake up. He didn't see Nori or Henrik in the pile of limbs. Hopefully everyone got enough sleep.

He rubbed his forehead, wincing as he touched the spot where the raven pecked him with its pale pinkish beak. Stupid bird. He still didn't understand how it got free in the first place.

"What do you want?" he asked, feeling grumpy and out of sorts.

It shuffled on its perch, spread its wings, and cawed again. Aleks slapped his hands over his ears. Its cries were too loud in the small space.

"Can someone shut that blasted thing up?" Geirr grumbled, shoving Filip's feet away from his face. "Worst alarm clock ever."

Christoffer laughed and stretched. "I'm sure there's something worse. Oh, I know. Imagine if Nori had woken you up instead of the bird."

Geirr pulled a face, suppressing a shudder. "That is worse. I can just picture her face leaning over me."

"Like a mare," Christoffer added, holding his hands out like claws.

"Giving a loud sniff," Filip said, making the sound.

"Don't be mean," Zaria scolded, yawning and stretching. "I know she can be trying. She gets on my nerves, too, but we don't have to make fun of her."

"Sure, Zaria," said Christoffer, slinging an arm around her neck. "She hasn't knocked you out either, unlike another irritating female we all know. So that's a plus, right?"

Zaria fake-punched him in the side, causing him to dance away. "Be nice!" he admonished.

"I will, if you will," she replied.

"I'm always nice," he countered. "You have to admit I'm right. Only a mare could be scarier than Nori."

Mares were creatures that looked like the humanoid monster that stalked the frightened protagonist in horror films. They had long, tangled, black hair; pale skin that nearly glowed in the dark; black, claw-like nails; and soulless black eyes. Mares terrorized their victims while they slept, feeding on nightmares and perhaps even giving them to their victims.

Unless one took the precaution of strategically hammering nails into the bed frame, mares were nigh unstoppable, for they could shapeshift into sand and slip into anyplace their victims hid. No house was safe. Aleks thanked God that they hadn't had to cross paths with any yet on their current adventure. Banshees were enough to deal with.

"Someone help me with this bird," he said, trying to grab the raven.

It squawked and flew up onto a cupboard. Aleks dragged a kitchen chair below it and climbed on top. The bird took off and landed on the sofa back. Geirr and Filip tried to pounce on it at the same time, just missing it and clunking heads together.

"Ow. You've got a hard head," Geirr complained, rubbing his forehead.

"You're one to talk, mate," Filip said wryly, rubbing his forehead, too. "Where did it go?"

"Over there," said Christoffer, pointing toward the small foyer. "It's by the door."

They raced after it and it took off, flying outside. Dim morning light lit the glade, painting it in soft hues. The raven circled above them calling to them to follow. "Eye-riii! Eye-riii!"

Aleks ran after it, spurring everyone else into motion. They chased it to the stables where they found Henrik and Nori harnessing a small group of winter-wyverns. Aleks stood in the doorway watching, until Nori spied him there. Christoffer plowed into his back, and they stumbled into the stable, the others soon joining them inside.

"You're up early," Henrik said, surprised at seeing them. "I was going to let you all sleep."

"This damn bird woke me up," said Aleks, jabbing his thumb at the smug raven. "Help us catch it."

"Interesting," said Henrik, glancing at the raven. "I traded the ravens with Silje for access to her stable of winter-wyverns."

"Stupid," Nori said, rolling her eyes. "White ravens are more valuable than winter-wyverns. They're far rarer and far cleverer."

Henrik shrugged. "It's more like a loan, and we needed transportation north."

"Loan?" asked Zaria.

Henrik gave a small hum and then said, "If any of the ravens bond with her or one of the elves, she can keep them. The same applies for the winter-wyverns and us. We'll swap back later when we return."

"It's still a bad trade," said Nori, but she grinned, patting her beast's neck. "These beauties, however, will get us to Jerndor faster than anything else we could do. I'm choosing this gorgeous chestnut here."

"I'm going to find something to catch that nuisance," said Geirr, indicating the raven. He wandered off, disappearing further inside the stables.

"Did you tell Silje about Trolgar?" asked Aleks, searching for something with a long pole among the tools by the door.

"We did, and about Fritjof, too. Silje doesn't remember any such dragon either," Henrik said. His blue eyes held deep concern. "How can a dragon wipe the memory of himself from our minds? It doesn't make any sense."

"Is she going to help the trolls? Or fight the dragon?" asked Zaria.

"She gave her word she would look into them both," said Nori with a disgusted huff. "Doesn't she realize there isn't time for 'looking into' it?"

"You first have to earn her trust," said Henrik.

"Doesn't she trust you?" Nori retorted. "That should be enough."

"I think we can reach it, if you climb on my shoulders, Zar-Zar," said Filip, focusing on the raven.

He bent down, and she took his hand, climbing up. She wobbled unsteadily as he rose to his feet. He didn't let go until he was fully upright. Zaria straightened, holding her arms akimbo for balance. Finding it, she turned to coax the raven down.

Filip dipped sideways under her shifting weight. Zaria shrieked, tipping over as she lost her balance. Filip caught her, staggering a little. The raven took off, calling out "Eye-riii!" and dove at Aleks' head. He ducked, waving his arms to ward it off. Geirr appeared, made a wild grab, and missed, bumping into Nori who shoved him away.

"Hold still," Henrik commanded, holding both his hands out to keep everyone in their place. "I think the raven has picked Aleks."

Aleks held his breath, amazed. Filip slowly set Zaria down onto her feet. Christoffer lowered a net he'd found from somewhere. Nori stroked the fur on the winter-wyvern she'd claimed. Everyone eyed the bird.

"Picked me?" Aleks asked, standing. "Whatever for?"

The raven made a cautious circle above their heads and then slowly descended. Aleks flinched away, causing it to rear back. He straightened, making eye contact with the thing. It stretched out its talons and found a perch on his shoulder. He winced a little under their sharp bite.

"I was right," said Henrik, lowering his hands. "Congratulations."

"I knew I didn't like you, little brother," Nori said, sighing. The sound was equal parts longing and jealousy.

Hesitantly, Aleks raised a hand to the raven. It clicked its beak in warning, but he forged ahead and made contact. With care, he stroked the cool white feathers on its chest. The bird leaned into his touch and closed its wintry blue eyes for a moment.

"Why are white ravens so special?" he asked.

"When they bond, they can be taught to speak, as you know," said Henrik, walking over to them. He raised a hand to pet the raven, but retracted it at the raven's angry warning call.

"Can't a parrot do that?" asked Christoffer. "That's not so special."

Nori shot him a glare. "Imbecile, he meant real speech, not mimicking."

Henrik nodded. "In addition, they guard their owner's secrets, know when their owner needs them, and can carry messages great distances."

"They also make great spies," Nori said. "Niffleheim hasn't seen a white raven since the well was lost and we were cut off from the world. Silje won't be happy that one of the five is coming with us."

Henrik turned back to the winter-wyvern he'd been harnessing when they had arrived in the stables. "Be that as it may, the raven has chosen. She shouldn't have set them free, if she wasn't willing to lose them to outsiders."

"What are you going to name it?" asked Geirr.

"I don't know," said Aleks, stroking its feathers with the backs of his knuckles. They were soft and silky. "I'll have to see what fits him."

The raven nipped angrily at his ear.

"Er, her?" he asked it, rubbing the tender spot.

The raven bobbed its head and settled back onto his shoulder. She crooned softly, as he returned to petting her feathers. Leaning into his touch, she raised a wing.

"She's protecting you already," Henrik said. "That's a good sign."

Something in Aleks' chest melted at the thought. The white raven was actually quite pretty, with a wintery-soft rosy hue to its beak and feet. She was his. He would take good care of her.

"Zaria, you'll be on Norwick," said Henrik, drawing Aleks' attention away from the raven. "He's trained, and I know he's tame. Plus, he loves you."

"Don't you want to ride on Norwick?" she asked.

"I figured we'd ride together," said Henrik, missing Filip's look of consternation. "Silje only gave us five winter-wyverns. Those plus Norwick make six, so two people would have to double-up anyway."

"I'm telling you this because I'm nice," Nori said, sounding anything but, which earned a snort from Christoffer. She shot him a glare and continued, "You should never be allowed to make trades. It is not your strong suit."

"It was my father's," Henrik said, tugging his hood lower. "I have to try following in his footsteps."

Zaria rested a hand on his shoulder. "You're your own person, Henrik. Hector would want you to find what makes you happy. You don't have to trade and wander around between the kingdoms like he did. He loved exploring and meeting people. Trading gave him a purpose."

"You got Master Brown to give you the birds in the first place – that's pretty good trading," said Christoffer. "You're not doing as bad as Nori says."

"We should get going," Henrik said, and Zaria let her hand drop.

"Finally, you're seeing things my way," Nori said, swinging up onto the saddle of her chestnut.

Christoffer climbed onto the back of a solid gray one. Aleks took the one Henrik had just finished saddling, a nice white one freckled with brown spots. The raven left him to fly alone. Geirr set aside his net and took a gray with a white patch around its eye, that Christoffer dubbed Patches.

Filip stared after Zaria and Henrik, watching as the Stag Lord helped her up behind him on Norwick. Aleks gave him a look of commiseration. Filip sighed and ran a hand through his hair, saying nothing. He climbed astride the last of the winter-wyverns, a brown male with white stripes.

They led the winter-wyverns from the stables and into the clearing. Edevart and Frida met them there, handing up their backpacks one at a time. The breath of the winter-wyverns created a hazy bank of fog in the morning air. It curled around the scene, cloaking everything it touched in white.

"Thank you for having us," said Zaria, leaning down to give Frida a kiss on the cheek.

"It was our pleasure," she said. "I've packed some extra cakes in your bags."

"We'll eat every one," Zaria said, nodding toward the boys. "I bet they'll be devoured by lunchtime."

Frida stepped back, smiling and waving her goodbyes. Edevart joined her, and together they saw them off. Zaria shrieked gaily as Norwick launched into the sky. Aleks and Filip took off, coming up on either side with Christoffer, Geirr, and Nori right behind them.

They turned themselves and headed north. The white raven joined them, flying just ahead of Aleks and his winter-wyvern. She ca-cawed and did a little swoop and spin. Aleks watched her enjoy the freedom of flight, stretching out her wings and gliding as softly as a cloud in the sky. She caught his eye and cried, "Eye-riii!" He smiled fondly after her.

Henrik turned to the side, calling out, "We should head to Jerndor."

"Do you know how to find it?" Filip asked. "We've only been inside the dwarf city."

Henrik shook his head. "I don't know the landmarks. I've never been there, not even underground. Nori?"

The wind snatched his words and carried them to her. The fairy shook her head. "I, too, have only been to the city underground."

"Could you find it, Aleks?" asked Geirr.

"Maybe," he said, frowning. "I can try."

"You'll find it," said Geirr confidently. "You always find what you're looking for."

He hoped that was still true. Aleks closed his eyes, feeling the wind blow in his hair, concentrating on the steady *whoomp whoomp whoomp* of the winter-wyvern's beating wings. He pictured Norway, thinking of the Varanger Peninsula and adjusted his wyvern to the right.

"We should be there sometime shortly after lunch," he said, opening his eyes, feeling his internal clock and navigation adjust. "The dwarves are about the same distance from the elves as the giants are."

The sun waxed strong, as the day wore on. For breakfast they stuffed themselves on crisp, red apples. Aleks kept adjusting their course, a little here, and a little there, following his intuition. Around midday

Zaria opened her backpack and passed out the cakes Frida had given them. They ate them midflight.

The flight was easygoing, and all of Norway passed by underneath. Shortly before landing Aleks spotted Christoffer sleeping again, slumped against the neck of his winter-wyvern. A spittle of drool blew backward from his mouth.

Aleks swerved his beast closer, shouting, "Wake up!"

Christoffer's wyvern dipped and rolled, jolting him awake. He clutched at the neck, and asked, "Are we there, yet?"

"Almost. I think its straight down there," Aleks said, pointing to a rocky plateau.

One after another they landed on the ground, on top of the rock-strewn formation. Aleks swung his leg over and hopped down. Filip hurried to get off his and help Zaria from the back of Norwick. Aleks hoped his friend would ask her out and soon. The last thing the group needed was a love triangle.

"I think I'm finally getting the hang of riding one of these," said Geirr, smiling widely, patting his beast. "I didn't fight vertigo once on the trip. That's progress!"

"That's great," said Christoffer. "You know, I never understood how you could fly airplanes when you didn't like heights."

Geirr shrugged. "I wanted to get over my fear. I thought taking lessons would help, which they did, at least when I was in a cockpit. This is progress."

"How do we get into the city?" asked Nori, peering at the flat rocks littering the top of the plateau. She stooped to pick one up, balancing it on one end. Dirt greeted her and she dropped the stone with a thud. "That's not the way."

Aleks looked around trying to figure out what had drawn him to this location. He searched the countryside. Nothing stood out. He peered over the edge of the plateau and saw a narrow stairway cut into the cliff face. It stopped halfway down on a thin ledge. Geirr wasn't going to like this.

"Down there," he said. "That's the way in."

Geirr peeked gingerly over the side and gulped. "I don't think I can climb down there. I haven't made that much progress."

"I'll see you down there," said Nori, brushing past the two and taking the rocky path at a lope.

Geirr took several steps away from the ledge and clung to the reins of the gray and white winter-wyvern he'd ridden. His eyes were wide with fear.

"I'll help you," said Aleks. "I'll go first. You just hang onto me and don't look over the side."

Zaria nodded and added, "I can use my magic to help you, too."

"How?" Geirr croaked, his dark skin quickly developing a pallor as sweat broke out at his temples.

"Why doesn't he just ride Patches to the ledge?" asked Christoffer. "That could work."

"How would he dismount?" Henrik asked. "That isn't the way for him to get down."

"Rope then?" offered Filip. "We could lower him to the ledge."

"No way," said Geirr. "Not for all the rubies in Jerndor. I'll just sit this out with, – what did you name my winter-wyvern, Christoffer?"

"Patches. Come on Geirr, don't wimp out," Christoffer said, dragging the protesting teen away from the beast.

"Easy for you to say, you daredevil. Let me go!" Geirr said, struggling.

"Don't force him," said Zaria, pushing Christoffer away. "You'll make it worse. Go down. Take Henrik and Filip with you."

She and Geirr watched them go. Henrik turned back and gave commands to the winter-wyverns to wait for them to return. Then he was gone.

Aleks stayed, took some rope, and wrapped it around his waist. He knotted it securely and then did the same around Geirr and Zaria, giving the last knot a sharp tug for good measure.

"Okay, we're all set to do this," said Aleks. "Ready?"

"No," Geirr said.

Zaria nudged him. "Yes. We're ready; you start and we'll follow. We'll go slowly. You can do it, Geirr."

"I can do it," Geirr said, swallowing hard.

Aleks stepped down, and down again. He stopped when the rope went taut. He looked behind him.

Geirr moaned. "Don't do that. Keep your eyes where you're going."

He raised an eyebrow. "Then you better start following me."

"Take one step at a time," Zaria said, nudging him again. "I'm right here. We've got you."

Geirr took a step down. Aleks turned around and took another step and another. He could hear Geirr behind him, mumbling to himself, and Zaria's constant stream of encouragement. Before they knew it, the trio was even with the others, stepping down onto the short ledge. Aleks unclipped his end of the rope. They'd made it.

Chapter Fourteen:
Well, Where Is It?

A weathered copper door towered above them. It could comfortably fit a giant, which as Christoffer pointed out was incredibly stupid, because what giant could or would take the human-sized stairs to get to it? What was the point? They knocked and waited for someone to come open it.

Aleks studied the door while they waited. It was cool-looking with its green patina and detailing. The whole thing was covered by an elaborate relief featuring

Vikings, longboats, dwarves, giants, and a long serpentine dragon. The dragon twisted all around the scene, attacking all and everything. It had twin tails, thin and twisted like cords, entwining around two ships, cracking them in half.

The face of the creature struck a chord with Aleks. He had the oddest sensation he had seen it up close before, but he couldn't follow the thought back to its source. It evaporated as he took in the wide mouth, filled with serrated teeth. The bridge of its nose was stunted, giving the dragon a squashed appearance. Surrounding its eyes and mouth were dozens of spikes. A crown of them even encircled its head.

It was probably a trick of the light, but every time Aleks looked away from the dragon's face its eyes seemed to glow yellow. When he refocused on the relief the eyes were merely green, a result of copper oxidizing. He opened his mouth to say something when Nori banged on the door. He got the impression this wasn't the first time she'd done so.

"This door should be manned," she said, sniffing with disdain. "Or at least patrolled. This would never have been left unguarded in Niffleheim."

"Says the fairy with an unguarded passage linking Niffleheim to Jerndor," Geirr muttered.

"That's different," said Nori, with a sniff. "Besides the dwarves guard their end of it."

"This place is rather inaccessible," Zaria said, leaning with her back against the door. "How often would they have visitors here?"

"Henrik, do you have the Gjallarhorn?" asked Filip. "Maybe we can call below to King Flein."

The Stag Lord shook his head. "I do, but I left it up top with the wyverns. I didn't think we'd need it."

Nori knocked again, ending the sequence with a sharp kick. "This is useless," she said, sinking against the door beside Zaria.

"What they need is a doorbell," said Christoffer, admiring the doors. "These carvings are wicked. I wonder who the dragon is."

"You're kidding me, right?" Nori asked, looking at him. She looked to the others and huffed. "It's Fritjof."

There was an implied 'Duh' following her words.

"We don't all have your truth gift," Aleks reminded her. "We don't remember him at all."

"Why does he have two tails?" asked Christoffer.

Nori looked behind her at the carving of the tails wrapping around the boats. She raised an eyebrow, her contempt clear. Christoffer colored angrily under her haughty gaze. Aleks wondered if he'd have to intervene to keep the peace.

After a moment, Nori relented and said, "His tails twine together like a rope. It's the ultimate level of surprise when he attacks because he can use them together on a single target or separately on multiple targets. He can do one or the other in a blink of an eye, so quickly you'd never see it coming. Wham! You're dead."

"Great," said Geirr dryly. "Who doesn't love it, when you're attacked on both sides?"

Aleks clapped Geirr on the back. "It's nice that you're so cheerful about all this."

"Ha. Ha," he muttered. "Hilarious. I'm being serious, though. When we finally catch up with this dragon, how are we supposed to fight it? Stand in a circle with our backs to each other?"

"That never works with him," said Nori.

A scuffling sound diverted their attention. Nori turned around and knocked again. "Hello? Answer the door! We can hear you back there."

The skittering increased and a small panel by their knees opened, revealing a blue face. It was another brownie. Aleks couldn't tell from its squished appearance, if it was male or female.

"Who goes there?" a high-pitched squeaky voice called out. It was definitely a female.

"I am Nori, daughter of Grimkell, the Ruler of the Autumn Court in Niffleheim. These are my estimable companions: Princess Zaria of the Under Realm; Stag Lord of the ellefolken; and our servants. We require passage back into the Niffleheim."

"Servants?" hissed Geirr. "I'd never work for her."

"Me either," Christoffer whispered back. "She's dreaming."

"The way is closed," said the brownie. She began to shut the panel.

"Madam Brown," Nori said tersely, slapping her hand against the panel, keeping it open. "You will let us in, and you will escort us to the Thief of Peace's Passage."

"The way is closed," repeated Madam Brown. Her face contorted as she struggled to shut the door.

"Why is it closed?" asked Henrik, bending down on one knee to be close to the brownie's face.

She ceased struggling and blinked at him, taking in his antlered cloak. "Stag Lord, I regret to tell you that Niffleheim is at war with Jerndor. The passage is closed to all outsiders. If your fairy friend entered within these walls, she would become a prisoner of war, which is a highly unpleasant experience, and despite her incivility I couldn't in good conscience let her inside to suffer such a fate."

"You lie," Nori hissed. "My father would never allow a war to break out with the dwarves."

"Didn't you tell me that your aunt and uncle overthrew him?" asked Aleks.

At this revelation, the brownie's eyes narrowed suspiciously. She studied them both with care.

"Even then he wouldn't allow it," Nori said, ignoring the brownie's sharp, beady gaze.

"He might not have had any choice," said Henrik.

The brownie wrinkled her nose and began shutting the panel again. "Good-bye."

Henrik stopped her this time, blocking the latch. "Madam Brown, you've been most helpful. May I trouble you for a little more of your time and wisdom. Can you tell us how the fighting broke out?"

Madam Brown considered him for a long minute. She sighed and opened the panel wide again. "Cornelia and Ytorm accused King Flein of kidnapping their niece and colluding with the Summer Court."

"I wasn't kidnapped," Nori said. "I'm right here. This is absurd."

"Be quiet," Henrik said, motioning her to silence. "Let Madam Brown finish telling us about your aunt and uncle."

"They've been quite unreasonable. King Flein tried diplomacy, but his patience finally snapped when Ytorm sent a troop into the passage to storm the mirrors."

Henrik touched his brow in thanks. "We appreciate you sharing this information."

"But we'd appreciate more an entrance into Jerndor," Nori said, looking down her nose at the brownie.

Madam Brown shot Nori an equally disdainful glare. "I'll not be doing that, even if you be the missing fairy that started this whole mess. It isn't safe."

"Looks like we're climbing back up," Aleks said to Geirr, knowing there was no good way to break the news to him.

His friend stared at him, his blue eyes filled with worry. Geirr gulped. "Of course we are." He looked at Madam Brown. "Please reconsider. I have a terrible fear of heights."

Madam Brown shot him a pitying look. "I'm afraid it is the only way up. Besides, you braved it to come down here. You can be brave again."

Aleks nudged him. "Zaria and I will guide you up again. It'll be easy."

"One more thing, Madam Brown," Henrik said, as the others began psyching themselves up to start the climb back to the top of the cliff. "Has King Flein left the mirrors intact?"

"For now," she said. "If you wish to prevent their destruction, you'd best hurry. King Flein has contemplated destroying them to be done with this senseless war."

"He can't," Nori said, stopping Aleks from following Geirr. "Tell her why Niffleheim needs those mirrors."

Aleks turned around to face the door, nodding toward the dragon carving. "Fritjof is back, and we're trying to stop him from escaping the Under Realm."

Madam Brown quirked her head to the side. "Who is Fritjof?"

"Not you, too," said Nori, aghast. She pointed at the dragon on the door. "That's Fritjof."

The brownie paled, studying the door. "I shouldn't let you in. I shouldn't. Your claim is unverified. That dragon can't be back." She stilled and glared at them.

"You said your father ruled Niffleheim. He doesn't. You lied. You say this dragon is back. You lie again. No admittance to liars."

The panel slammed shut before Henrik could stop her. Nori knocked again, but the brownie didn't come back. She beat on the carvings and kicked the door, until Henrik dragged her away.

"Don't let them destroy the mirrors!" Nori shouted, wrenching herself free of Henrik's hold.

Aleks grabbed her by the shoulder and shook her. "Nori, there's nothing we can do from here. We must get going."

"Where to?" she asked. "There's nowhere else. We're doomed. It's all your fault!"

"My fault?" Aleks asked. "How is it my fault?"

"You just had to go to Trolgar," she said.

"We were captured trying to find you," he said, trying to keep his patience. "You're the one who ran off."

Her mouth tightened into an angry moue. "You just *had* to help them."

"You're blaming us for rescuing imprisoned children?" Aleks asked, scoffing. "You're a piece of work. If we left you here, you'd deserve it."

"Aleks," Henrik said, disapprovingly. "We need to catch up to the others. Leave this line of talk behind, the both of you. It's nobody's fault."

Nori lapsed into a fuming silence. Aleks spun on his heel and started up the stairs two at a time, leaving her to follow. Ahead, Geirr and Zaria were climbing painfully slowly. They hadn't made it very far. Geirr had a death grip on her hand, resisting her every attempt to hurry him along. It was a good thing because Aleks had been arguing and not paying attention. He should have clipped himself to them again for safety.

"Just keep climbing, man," Aleks said, from a few steps below.

His words startled Geirr, who looked back over his shoulder at him. Aleks saw his eyes widen and his grip tighten. He wobbled dangerously, ignoring Zaria's frantic calls for him to look away and keep going. Aleks dashed up the stairs just as Geirr pitched sideways and fell off, taking Zaria with him.

"NO!" Aleks shouted, diving for them. He landed painfully against the edge.

He grasped Zaria's collar, halting her and Geirr's downward plunge. They slammed hard into the cliff wall. Aleks found himself sliding dangerously forward under their combined weight.

"Don't let me fall," Geirr moaned. He began praying, tightening his grip on Zaria's hand. Her fingers were practically white.

"A little help here," she gasped. "He's slipping."

"No, oh no, no, no, no," said Geirr, scrabbling to keep his hold.

He slipped and screamed, scrambling for the rope. Zaria grunted as his weight pulled her down again.

"You dropped me," he accused.

"Your hands were sweaty," Zaria said defensively, huffing under the strain of being pulled in two directions.

"Stop it," Aleks grunted, trying to pull them up. "Don't argue."

The stitching in Zaria's collar ripped. She and Geirr squeaked as they dropped an inch lower. A second hand reached out and grasped Zaria's collar. Aleks looked over to find Henrik staring stonily ahead, sweat beading his brow.

"We have to pull them up," he said.

Aleks nodded, blowing his bangs off his face. "Together on three. One. Two. Three!"

He and Henrik hauled on her collar, dragging Zaria and Geirr up one precious inch at a time. The fabric ripped further along the seam, coming undone faster and faster. Panic tore through him as Zaria and Geirr dropped down another few inches. The collar would give way before they rescued them.

"Lift up your hands," Aleks grunted, sweat beading down the tip of his nose. "Trust us to grab you."

"Those are words I don't want to hear right now," moaned Geirr.

Zaria raised her arms, careful not to dislodge their hold on her collar. She closed her eyes tight. "Okay. I'm ready."

"I'm not!" shouted Geirr as the fabric ripped more, dropping them another inch.

"No choice," grunted Henrik. "Now!"

He and Aleks let go of Zaria's shirt and caught at her arms, gaining a hold on her wrists. She clasped their wrists in return and they stood, hauling both of them upward. Henrik released Zaria to grab the rope connecting her to Geirr.

Aleks joined him, and they pulled their friend the rest of the way up. The four of them collapsed against the cliff wall, panting from exertion. That had been close. Too close. He swallowed.

As soon as his pulse began to slow, Aleks opened his eyes to spy Geirr climbing the stairs on his hands and knees, scrambling for the top, hampered by the rope that bound him and Zaria together. It was tangled around his legs and ankles. Aleks stood and raced after him, unclipping him, so he wouldn't drag Zaria forward. Then he hoisted Geirr upright, and pushed him the last few steps to the top. They surged up and over together, collapsing onto the ground in a boneless heap.

"Don't do that again," Aleks said, punching Geirr's arm. "Keep it together next time."

"There's a next time?" Geirr moaned. "What did I do to deserve that?"

Aleks huffed, feeling the edges of hysteria creep over him. He'd almost lost two of his friends on this dumb quest. Why were they even on it? Why couldn't grownups take care of saving the world? If they did, then he and his friends could be playing board games, going to movies, and planning dates to the school dance. Normal teenage stuff.

"What did any of us do to deserve it?" he asked, sitting up and slinging his arms over his knees. "Dragons are too big of a problem to handle on our own. It's crazy to try."

"That's the truth," said Nori, coming up behind Zaria and Henrik as they reached the top. "What do you think I've been trying to do all this time? I've been trying to gather an army, but nobody listens to me."

"Why didn't you help us save them?" Aleks asked, sobering. "You just stood there."

"What could I do that you two weren't already doing?" she asked, stalking over to her waiting wyvern. "Come on. There's only one way left into Niffleheim now."

"What way is that?" asked Henrik.

"The Lost Well," Nori said primly. "Now you can't refuse to take me there."

"Let's get there while there's still daylight left," sighed Aleks, because of course, the only way left into Niffleheim was the one way they shouldn't take his sister.

"Right, well, let's get going then," said Filip, offering a hand to both Geirr and Aleks. They stood groaning in protest at sore muscles.

"Why does it matter if it's daylight again?" asked Christoffer, hauling himself into the saddle. "I can't remember."

"The well is only findable during the day, at dusk to be precise. It disappears at night," said Zaria.

"That's right," he said. "I remember now. The Thief of Peace's Passage had a similar time constraint."

Zaria nodded, giving Norwick a tender pat on the nose. "It closes on Niffleheim's side at dawn."

She hopped onto the winter-wyvern's back and Henrik joined her a moment later, securing the reins. Aleks judged the sun's height in the sky and got onto his winter-wyvern. He stroked the white and brown spotted fur, soothing his nerves. Closing his eyes, he focused on the Lost Well.

He didn't want to take Nori to it, knowing she would use it for nefarious purposes in the future, but it couldn't be helped. They would just have to find a way to prevent her from using the well to claim all of Niffleheim as her own.

He zeroed in on the well's location before opening his eyes. He caught Zaria's gaze, and she smiled encouragingly at him, pulling a reluctant one from him in return. "Follow me," he said, and launched into the sky.

He tucked into the warm furry neck, spinning his winter-wyvern into a spiral. Flying with the wind in his hair settled him. It blew all his worries away and cleared his muddied thoughts. He let go of it all and laughed, letting the joy of it carry him, delighting in the raven's happy "Eye-riii!" as she flew beside him.

They would find the well and reach Niffleheim by dinnertime. Their trip to Jerndor had only been a little delay.

As they soared above rainbow-colored clouds, soft as cotton candy, he kept his eye on the ground. At one point he spotted a wild reindeer herd streaking across the terrain and later, he saw a flock of birds take flight. He led them down as the sun lowered on the horizon, the bottom half barely touching the edges of the earth.

"We're here," he said, alighting as the others landed all around him.

He tossed the reins over the saddle and went to help Zaria down. Reaching her before Filip did, Aleks left the blond to stare at them uselessly. Christoffer began poking around, looking this way and that. Nori grinned at them all, giving Aleks the creeps. Her grin disappeared at Henrik's unwelcome words.

"Are you sure we're in the right spot?" he asked.

Aleks nodded. "Of course I'm sure. I can always find a place I've been to before."

Henrik nodded politely, but his expression remained unchanged. "I don't see it anywhere."

"What do you mean you don't see it?" demanded Nori. She spun around and poked Aleks in the chest. "Well, where is it?"

Aleks pushed her hand away and rubbed the spot. "It's right here. I know it." He tapped his forehead.

"Is it hidden?" asked Nori. "Did it move?"

"It's not like it could walk away," said Aleks, rolling his eyes. He walked around his winter-wyvern gesturing at the space behind it. "See? It's right there…."

Aleks stared at the empty space, dumbstruck. The well should be right there. He looked at the sun, still hanging low in the sky and back to the spot.

"It has to be there. Maybe we missed it and it'll be back tomorrow evening," he said.

"That's impossible," said Nori bitingly. Her face splotched red from fury. "It's still dusk now."

Aleks gritted his teeth, feeling color creep up his neck. "We're in the right spot."

"Is it possible you could be wrong?" asked Zaria, laying a hand on his arm.

"That's never happened to him before," said Christoffer, taking down his backpack. "Maybe Aleks is right about the well disappearing because of how low the sun is in the sky. Maybe it's dawn when the well appears, and we mixed up our times with the well and the passage. I can't remember. Can you?"

"You're wrong, and so is he," hissed Nori. "It appears at dusk. Where is the well little brother?"

"I don't know, okay?" he snapped, shocking them all. "I don't know."

"You really are a changeling," she spat, and the words landed like a slap against his face.

Epilogue: Lost Again

Dread lined his stomach like lead. Aleks spun around taking in their surroundings. Everything seemed right, from the grassy hills to the forest at a distance. The well should be right here.

The fact that it wasn't troubled him immensely. His sense of direction couldn't be this wrong. Sure, it had been on the fritz these last few days, but this? His inner compass never had been so far off. What was happening to him? Where was that blasted well?

"Lost again," Nori muttered, taking the bag with her belongings off her winter-wyvern. "I can't believe it. What else can go wrong?"

"We should settle in for the night and check the dawn theory in the morning," said Filip. "I'll help you with your tent, Zar-Zar."

"Thanks, Filip," she said, handing it to him. She looked at Aleks. "It'll be okay. You're never wrong. We'll find the well in the morning."

"What if I am wrong?" he asked, stress making his voice crack.

"Then we'll figure it out," she said. "We always do."

"I hope you're right," he said, running a hand through his hair. "There's no other option left to get to Niffleheim. I don't know what'll happen if we can't find the well."

Geirr snorted. "Death by dragon I would expect."

"You're such a worrywart," said Christoffer. "That's only the worst that could happen. There's other bad stuff that could happen first."

"You're right," Geirr said. "We could run into the Wild Hunt again, or be eaten by wild bears, or freeze to death from an unexpected snowstorm, or stomped on by traveling giants."

"Gee, thanks," said Aleks. "That's comforting."

"Only trying to help," said Christoffer. "Cheer up. You might be human quicker than you thought you'd be, and isn't that what you always wanted?"

It was, and that was the crux of his problems. What if he'd wished so hard to be human, he'd done this to himself? That was the worst thing he could imagine. How could he be of any use to his friends if he had lost the one talent he did have? How could he face them and tell them he was the cause of all their troubles?

Aleks didn't know the answers to any of it. He pitched his tent, not daring even to contemplate the disasters and pitfalls that lay ahead. He wasn't confident at all that they could face them, because he wasn't confident in himself. Not anymore.

Who was Aleks Mickelsen without his fey magic? Useless, that's what. He was nothing but a freeloading waste of space. He was just an ordinary changeling with nothing to his name and nothing to recommend him. It was a freaking disaster.

Zaria touched his arm, pulling him from his downward spiral. "We'll figure it out," she repeated quietly. "The well won't be lost forever. We'll find it."

Thanks for Reading

Thank you for reading Aleks Mickelsen's story! If you would, please take a moment to leave a review on Amazon or Goodreads. It would mean the world to me, and every time someone does leave a review a new winter-wyvern is born. Who wouldn't love to have their own Norwick? In all seriousness, your opinions help other readers discover the enchanting world of Zaria Fierce and beckon them to join the adventure.

DIGITAL DESKTOP BACKGROUNDS
FEATURING ARTWORK FROM THE SERIES

Sign up for my new releases mailing list and get 10 free desktop backgrounds featuring artwork by Eoghan Kerrigan from the Zaria Fierce Series.

Go here to get started: http://keiragillett.com/free-download/

Up Next

Aleks Mickelsen and the Call of the White Raven

Get a sneak peek of the next book in the Zaria Fierce world, featuring Aleks' adventures:

http://keiragillett.com/book/white-raven/

About the Author: Keira Gillett

When she's not working or writing, Keira Gillett loves to play tabletop games. Nearly every week Keira gets together with her friends to play. It's no wonder she invented a game of her own for her Zaria Fierce Series. You can find the rules to this game within the second book and make your own version of it through a tutorial on her website. She'd loved to hear from you! Why not send her a picture of you and a friend playing the game?

Find her at http://keiragillett.com/

About the Artist: Eoghan Kerrigan

Eoghan Kerrigan is an illustrator from Kildare, Ireland who draws primarily fantasy characters and creatures. He studied illustration in Ballyfermot College of Further Education and has produced work for various independent projects. He has two cats and a soft spot for trolls.

Find him at http://eoghankerrigan.blogspot.ie/

About the Cartographer: Kaitlin Statz

Kaitlin Statz grew up in many different places but currently lives in Sarasota, FL with her partner Travis and their young dog, Eezo. She attended New College of Florida and the University of Oxford for a life in the sciences before returning to her true love, art. She started her work as Statz Ink in 2015 and has been creating art ever since.

Find her at http://www.statzink.com/

73381794R00164

Made in the USA
Columbia, SC
12 July 2017